"I know you don't want to talk about the past, but we've got to clear the air."

"I don't see the point, Maria."

"We just have to get it out of the way once and for all. Then we don't have to worry about stumbling over the subject down the line."

Grady gritted his teeth, then forced himself to relax. "So what do you want to do?"

"I want to set the record straight about Nina."

"What's there to say about a woman who ran off and left her husband and children? A good wife and mother wouldn't do that."

"It doesn't mean she wasn't a good mother."

"In my opinion, it does."

"Well, maybe you were a..." Maria's voice trailed off.

"Maybe I was what?"

"Nothing," Maria said, shaking her head. "I just wanted you to understand that no one's all good or all bad."

"So I'm just supposed to forget what she did? She ran off with another man, and *you* let her."

Books by Merrillee Whren

Love Inspired

The Heart's Homecoming #314
An Unexpected Blessing #352
Love Walked In #378
The Heart's Forgiveness #406

MERRILLEE WHREN

is the winner of a 2003 Golden Heart Award for best inspirational romance manuscript, presented by Romance Writers of America, and in 2004, she made her first sale to Steeple Hill Books. She is married to her own personal hero, her husband of twenty-nine years, and has two grown daughters. She has lived in Atlanta, Boston, Dallas and Chicago, but now makes her home on one of God's most beautiful creations, an island off the east coast of Florida. When she's not writing or working for her husband's recruiting firm, she spends her free time playing tennis or walking the beach, where she does the plotting for her novels.

Merrillee loves to hear from readers. You can contact her through her Web site at www.merrilleewhren.com.

The Heart's
Forgiveness
Merrillee Whren

Steeple
Hill®

Published by Steeple Hill Books™

STEEPLE HILL BOOKS

Steeple
Hill®

ISBN-13: 978-0-373-87442-2
ISBN-10:   0-373-87442-1

THE HEART'S FORGIVENESS

Copyright © 2007 by Merrillee Whren

www.SteepleHill.com

Printed in U.S.A.

"Therefore I tell you, whatever you ask for in prayer, believe that you have received it, and it will be yours. And when you stand praying, if you hold anything against anyone, forgive him, so that your Father in heaven may forgive you your sins."

—*Mark* 11:24–25

This story is dedicated to my daughter and son-in-law, Kara and Joe O'Brien.

I want to thank my daughter, Danielle, and my friends, Piper John and Karen Potter, for their help with this project.

I would also like to thank Stephanie Hardin, who helped me understand the work of an administrator of an assisted living facility, Ronda Wells, M.D., who helped me with information about hypothermia, and Alan Botzheim of the Pend Oreille County sheriff's department, who gave me information related to search and rescue. All mistakes are mine.

And I give special thanks to my husband, Bob, for his encouragement and the perfect suggestion for a plot point for this story.

Chapter One

The dreaded day had arrived. Maria Sanchez was finally facing Grady Reynolds, who sat across from her at a shiny cherry conference table. Twisting her hands in her lap, she gathered her courage and weighed her words. "Let's just get the past out of the way."

Grady narrowed his gaze. "And what do you mean by that?"

The forced smile Maria was trying to hold in place faded as she read displeasure in the frown that creased his brow. "You know what I mean. About what happened when your wife died."

"I don't want to talk about Nina's death. It doesn't have anything to do with here and now."

"Then you won't let it interfere with our working together."

"No. I believe we can make this a smooth transition. The past won't interfere."

She should have been satisfied with that answer, but his expression made her doubt his willingness to put their history behind them. "Okay, but why do I get the feeling you still hold some resentment?"

"Because I do. But it won't be a problem." He stared at her, his blue eyes and the set of his shoulders conveying his discomfort.

Could she convince him that tiptoeing around the past was only going to make things difficult later on? "Don't you think we should clear the air?" she asked.

"Rehashing what happened isn't going to change anything." His chin jutted out. "So let's drop it."

Crossing her arms, Maria pressed her lips together in an effort to keep from saying something she'd regret. The last time they had spoken, the day of his wife's funeral more than four years earlier, his cruel and untrue accusations about Maria's part in his wife's betrayal had crushed her heart. And she had made no attempt to defend herself against the grieving, angry man.

Now he didn't want to talk. Possibly, he was right, but Maria feared his view of what had taken place would interfere with their working relationship. Maybe she just needed to give it time—to get to know him again and see how things went. "If that's how you feel, then I won't discuss it. After all, I haven't talked about it since then. Why should I start now?"

"I appreciate your silence." Sitting back in his chair, he seemed to relax. "I'm trying to put the past behind me. Talking about it just resurrects the whole mess."

How could she respond? She believed a person had to get the past out in the open, not shove it in some corner. But that was *her* way of dealing with the past, not Grady's. With God's help, she'd try to see things Grady's way.

Maria watched as he opened a folder with the JMR

Charitable Foundation logo on it. He looked much the same as he had the last time she'd seen him, except that the lines around his blue eyes had deepened. His light brown hair was still cut in the same short style and his charcoal-gray suit showed off his broad shoulders.

She had forgotten what a handsome man he was. Or maybe she had never seen him as attractive, because of his wife's complaints that he was a man who cared more about his job than his family. That had struck a chord within her because her father had been that way, too.

Good looks couldn't cover a flawed character. But no one else seemed to hold the opinion that he was flawed in any way. Everyone else thought he was wonderful. Ever since Jillian Lawson, her boss, had hired him as the administrator of the new assisted-living facility, everyone had sung the praises of the high-powered attorney.

Maria had been fretting about this day ever since she heard the news. Trying to manufacture some confidence about working with Grady, she opened her portfolio and pulled out several brochures. "Here's the promotional material."

Still not meeting her gaze, he picked up one of the brochures and studied it. He motioned to the other brochures on the table. "Could you bring me up to speed on the opening?"

"Okay," Maria said, and proceeded to tell him about the program that the hospital auxiliary had planned for the opening.

"Sounds like everything's in order," he said when she'd finished.

"Yes, it is. We have residents ready to move in as soon as they give us a certificate of occupancy."

"When do you expect that to happen?"

"As soon as we pass the final inspection." Standing, she opened a folder and spread its contents on the table. "Here's a list of the inspections."

He joined her and glanced at the papers, then looked at her. "In a week?"

"Yes." Despite the past conflicts between her and Grady, she had to admit that having him on board made her job a lot easier. He could deal with the assisted-living facility, and she could now concentrate on her own responsibilities with the foundation.

"There's nothing like plunging into the job," he said.

"It'll keep you busy." Was he the same workaholic he'd been when Nina was alive? Hoping to gain insight into his present circumstances, Maria asked, "Where are your girls?"

"Amanda and Kelsey are staying with Nina's mother. I'm going back at the end of the week to get them. They aren't very excited about leaving California and all their friends."

"I can understand that. It's hard for kids to move. Where are you staying while you're here?"

Grady straightened the papers in the folder, then glanced at her. "At Clay's. Little brother's letting me stay in his apartment, since his family went with him on his consulting job."

Maria's heart sank. "I guess Clay told you I live in the upstairs apartment."

"Yeah, he mentioned it."

"You're staying there now?" she asked, wondering how she would deal with working with him and having him live so close, too. But he didn't seem bothered, at all. "I didn't see your car. How did I miss you?"

"I got into town after midnight and got up very early this morning to come to the office."

"Are you planning to rent the apartment after Clay and Beth move out?"

"Yeah, until we find something more permanent." He picked up one of the brochures and put it in his brief-case. "And it'll have to be soon, because I'm not sure how long the girls can survive sharing a room. Sometimes there's no love lost between them. Maybe it's the age difference."

"I wouldn't know. I didn't have a sister, just brothers. Four of them. Growing up, I often wished for a sister."

"I don't know." He shook his head. "Sometimes when my girls fight with each other, I think they wish they didn't have a sibling."

"They'll outgrow that." Maria remembered the last time she'd seen Amanda and Kelsey. Amanda had been nine, Kelsey only four. Now Amanda was a teenager. Hard to believe. "So they're not looking forward to the move?"

"No, but I bribed them. I told them they could learn to ski and ride horses." He smiled wryly, and a dimple appeared in his right cheek.

Maria didn't want to admit this man was absolutely gorgeous when he looked at her that way. And she'd been worried about not getting along with him? Now she had to worry about gaping at him when he entered the room. She gave herself a mental shake, reminding herself that his good looks wouldn't make up for the way he'd treated her.

"It'll be nice to see them again. I'm sure they've grown a lot since…" She bit her lip and glanced out the window. Here was the past again, intruding even when the subject seemed safe.

He finished her sentence for her. "Since their mother died."

"Yeah, since Nina died." Turning, Maria looked at him. What must it be like for those little girls to grow up without a mother? Her heart ached for them. "I wanted to know how they were coping. I prayed for them. And for you."

He stared back, his expression blank. "Maybe your prayers helped them, but they didn't do much for me."

"Prayers always help in some way."

"Maybe you think so."

"Yes, I do."

He gripped the back of the chair, his knuckles white. "Well, I don't."

"Even if you don't agree with me about prayer, I think you have to agree that the past is going to be an issue for us. All I did was ask about your girls, and there it was. The past."

Silence filled the room. Reading animosity in Grady's gaze, Maria turned away again to look out the window at the streets of the town of Pinecrest. A cloud momentarily cast a shadow across the landscape. What should she say now? She and Grady were the only ones who knew the awful truth about the death of his wife. Not even Clay knew about her affair with another man. And as far as Maria was concerned, no one ever needed to know.

Still, she wanted answers about why Grady was willing to work with her when he'd told her back then that he never wanted to see her again. Did she dare ask? *God, please help me say the right things. I don't want to alienate this man.*

Maria pivoted on her heel and faced him. "Why did you take this job when you knew I was working here?

You made it quite clear at Nina's funeral that you didn't approve of me."

Before he could answer, a jangling ring captured their attention. She glanced at the phone on the conference table, then back at him. With a sigh, she picked up the receiver. "Maria Sanchez. May I help you?" She paused and listened. "I see. I'll take care of it right away."

"Problems?"

"Yes, with the inspection." She gathered her papers and shoved them into her portfolio. "We need to go over to the site right away."

"What's wrong?"

"The plumbing. They'll show us when we get there." Maria sighed again. "I'm not sure how this will affect the people who are ready to move in and the opening celebration. We've built in extra time, but if this turns into something major, all those plans may have to be axed. That's the last thing we need."

"We'll get it worked out." Grady picked up his briefcase and followed her into the hallway.

"I hope you're right." She turned to look at him. "Did Jillian issue you a hard hat?"

He shook his head. "Do I need one?"

"Yes, when we get to the site. I keep mine in my car, but I have an extra in my office. I'll get it. And I'll get you a list of phone numbers for the contractors you'll be dealing with on the project."

"Great." He held up his briefcase and the brochures. "I need to put this stuff away and make a phone call before we go."

"Okay. I'll come down to your office after I pick up the hard hat."

Minutes later, Maria walked down the corridor, her

footsteps echoing in the quiet. The door to Grady's office was open, and she hesitated before entering. With his back to the door, he was standing in front of his office window and talking on a cell phone. Not wanting to interrupt his conversation, she stepped away. Even at a distance, she could hear his part of the exchange.

"I have to leave the office. I'm not sure when I'll be back. So if you need me, you can reach me on my cell phone." Then there was silence. Maria moved toward the door, but came to a sudden stop when she heard his voice again. "I love you, too. I miss you. I'll call you when I get home. Bye."

Maria wondered about the object of his affection. His kids? A girlfriend? Shaking off the speculation, she knocked lightly on the door frame and poked her head into the room. "Ready?"

Turning, he shoved the cell phone into his pocket. "Sure."

"Here's your hard hat," she said, noticing that he had discarded his tie and suit coat. It made him seem more approachable. Maybe it was a sign that their working relationship could get off to a good start.

"Thanks." Smiling, he took the hard hat and draped his coat and tie over his arm. "That was my girls on the phone."

"How are they?" Maria didn't want to think about her relief that it wasn't a girlfriend. She forced herself to think about something other than the way his smile made her feel.

He closed his office door. "Fighting, as usual."

"Didn't you fight with your brothers and sister when you were growing up?

Shrugging, he headed for the exit. "Could be, but I really don't remember fighting like that."

"I had some really awful fights with my older brothers, but we're all friends now. Though they still think of me as their *little* sister."

He looked down at her and grinned. "I can understand why."

She met his gaze. Although she was five and a half feet tall, he still stood a head taller than she did. He kept grinning at her. She glanced away. "Just because you're tall, that doesn't mean I'm little."

She strode quickly across the parking lot. His good-natured friendliness was something she hadn't expected. She knew this man as stern and standoffish. Why was he suddenly acting like they were friends? Was he just trying to make the best of their working relationship?

He laughed as he matched her pace. "Seems you're a little sensitive about your brothers' kidding."

"Maybe." She punched the keyless remote to unlock her car, she opened the back door and placed her computer case and hard hat on the seat. Then she turned to Grady, who was still grinning at her, and forced herself to smile at him. "We might as well ride together."

Grady glanced in Maria's direction as she pulled out of the parking lot. What was she thinking? Had the construction problems made her forget her unanswered question? He hadn't forgotten it. He'd tried to lighten the mood, but he'd sensed wariness in her response. He probably wasn't handling this well, at all.

He'd thought leaving his hometown and settling in this quiet, little town would mean leaving the past behind, as well. Somehow he'd made himself believe Maria wouldn't mention the hostility at Nina's funeral, but she'd brought it up without hesitation. How was he going to deal with it?

Even though he reported to Jillian Lawson, the founder of the charitable foundation, Maria wielded a lot of influence in the organization. Her navy blue power suit reminded him that she was a no-nonsense businesswoman. Animosity between them wouldn't help their working relationship. He didn't want to see disapproval over their last encounter in her dark chocolate-brown eyes. He'd thought being around her again wouldn't be a problem, but he'd been wrong. All the pain surrounding his wife's death had come rushing back like the gray clouds gathering just above the horizon in the western sky.

When Maria stopped at the red light in the middle of town, she looked his way. "I'd still like to know why you took this job when you knew I worked for Jillian."

Grady glanced at her for a moment, then turned to look out the window at the drugstore, post office and gas station on the main street. Had she been reading his thoughts? He wished he could escape her scrutiny, but he couldn't run away from the question. "I didn't know you still worked for Jillian," he replied, without looking at her. "I thought you'd left your position with the foundation when she moved her office here."

"I did take a year's leave of absence at the time of the move, but technically I still worked for Jillian. I had the opportunity to spend a year helping with one of the foundation's mission projects in El Salvador. Jillian urged me to go and promised that my job would be waiting for me when I returned."

"I've heard a lot of good things about Jillian and her foundation." He finally looked at Maria, but she was looking straight ahead when the light turned green.

"Jillian's one of the best friends I've ever had. I can't tell you what she means to me." She glanced his way for a moment, then turned her gaze forward again as she drove past the Pinecrest Café.

The disapproval he had been so worried about wasn't in her eyes. Instead, they shone brightly. With tears? He wasn't sure. Maybe it was the sunlight filtering through the clouds. He'd been prepared to continue despising her, but something tugged at his heart when she blinked and said, "You'll like working for her."

"That's what Clay said when he persuaded me to apply for this job."

"And you thought I was gone?"

"That's right." Grady nodded. "Last Thanksgiving, when I told Clay I was planning to close the law firm, he suggested I talk to Jillian about the assisted-living facility. When I met with her, she had me convinced to take the job in an instant."

A genuine smile curved Maria's generous lips. "Jillian *is* quite persuasive when it comes to her projects."

Grady nodded. "Especially the Alzheimer's unit."

"Yes, since her mother suffers from the disease." The breeze from the open window blew a strand of sable-brown hair across Maria's face. She reached up and pushed it behind one ear. "Why would you close the law firm?"

Grady furrowed his brow. How did he answer that question? There were lots of reasons. But he couldn't tell her about the most pressing one.

He didn't want to explain that he'd found a nearly empty bottle of vodka in Amanda's closet. She'd insisted it belonged to a friend, but Grady didn't know whether to believe her. And even if it did belong to a friend, that was a good enough reason to consider moving. She needed different friends.

Looking down, he rubbed his forehead. "It was a family decision. After Dad died, we kids kept the firm going. But after my sister had her first child, she didn't want to work full time. My brother Trent was tired of the long days. He wanted to teach at a nearby college. And Clay was never interested in being part of the firm. So it was a mutual decision to finish the cases we had, then close."

"This will be a different kind of work for you."

Grady wondered what she meant by that. Did she think he didn't have the necessary qualifications? "Yes, but many of my cases were in the health-care industry."

"I know, but you'll be seeing it from a different perspective now. Jillian told me about your experience. That's why she was excited about hiring you."

"But you don't share her excitement?"

Maria shook her head. "I didn't say that. I just thought you would've changed your mind when you found out I still worked for Jillian. Clay must've told you."

Grady laughed halfheartedly. "Yeah, after I had gone on and on about this being the perfect opportunity. I couldn't very well back out then."

"You could've," she said, raising an eyebrow. "If the girls don't want to move and you've got reservations about working with me, seems to me it wouldn't be worth it to take the job."

Grady wondered just how much he could reveal about his reasons for wanting to leave his hometown. "Yeah, but I decided having a good job was more important than worrying about you. And I needed to get the girls away from Nina's mother."

Maria frowned. "Why would you want to deprive the girls of their grandmother?"

Grady knew as soon as the words had left his mouth that he had said way too much. How was he going to explain? What was there about this woman that had him explaining himself when there was no need? And now she was expecting an answer.

"I'm not." Pressing his fingers to his forehead, he searched for the right words. "I just can't go on pretending Nina was a fine, upstanding woman who met a tragic death. When her mother starts praising Nina to Amanda and Kelsey—and wants me to give affirmation to what she says—it kills me. I don't want to denigrate Nina in front of the girls, but I hate pretending she was a wonderful person."

"She was a good mother," Maria said, her voice full of conviction.

"In your opinion." He shook his head. "I don't want to talk about Nina. It won't accomplish anything."

The hum of the motor filled the silence as Maria turned onto the highway that took them to the assisted-living facility on the far edge of town. He hoped there would be no more conversations about Nina or anything to do with the past. Maybe taking this job had been a bad idea after all. But he couldn't back out now. Jillian was counting on him. Too many things had been set in motion. He had sold his house in California. There was no turning back. And besides, he always fulfilled his obligations.

Once the facility was opened, he would move his office there, and he probably wouldn't see Maria very often. Right now, he needed her expertise to make the transition into the job. Her help was vital. Like today, with the inspectors and contractors. He could deal with Maria in the few weeks they would be working together on this endeavor. Or could he? Would the past continue to haunt them? He was beginning to have second thoughts about his adamant refusal to talk about Nina. Maybe he should find out why Maria had helped his wife with her betrayal.

He glanced Maria's way. His stomach lurched at the thought of discussing Nina. He didn't have the courage today. Besides, Maria had slowed the car to turn into the newly paved parking lot at the facility. Landscapers scurried around cutting and trimming the grass and planting shrubs along the foundation of the building. There wasn't enough time for a discussion now.

After Maria got out of the car, she stared at him, her dark eyes filled with worry. "Let's hope this turns out to be a small problem with a quick solution."

"That's exactly what I was thinking." He turned and strode up the walk. With every step he realized he wanted to take away her worry. Why did he want to do that? To prove to Maria—and to himself—that he was the right man for this job?

Maria hurried after Grady. His long strides carried him to the front door in a few steps. He opened it and waited for her to go inside. He even smiled. A good thing.

She didn't want to think about their disagreement over the past. That was the last thing she needed to be thinking about. They were both professionals. They could work together no matter the circumstances.

The smell of fresh paint greeted them as they stepped into what would eventually be the reception area. The clean fragrance of new construction filled the air. They donned their hard hats. The building looked complete, ready for furnishings and people, but nothing more would happen until all the inspections were done.

Maria glanced around, then turned to Grady. "The inspector said he'd meet us by the front door. Where is he?"

"Right here." A small, wiry man wearing a white hard hat and carrying a clipboard hurried toward them.

After a flurry of introductions, the inspector showed them several apartments where the plumbing wasn't up to code because the hot and cold faucets were reversed. Maria watched with reluctant appreciation as Grady took charge, making phone calls and taking notes. His charm and persuasive manner had people hopping to do whatever he said. Maria had never seen him work in the courtroom, but she was sure he had used these same skills to win many cases.

When Grady had finished talking with the inspector and making arrangements for a new inspection in a couple of days, they shook hands and the inspector left.

Shoving his cell phone into his pocket, he looked at Maria. "Well, that wasn't too bad."

"Yeah." Maria glanced at her watch. "Thankfully, that didn't take much time. I've got a meeting at four o'clock. I need to get back to the office."

Grady surveyed the room. "I'm going to hang around and wait for the plumbing contractor. That'll give me a chance to take a tour of the place. I'll catch a ride back to the office with someone."

"Sure. See you later." Relieved not to have to deal with Grady on her way back, Maria hurried out of the building. As she drove away, she caught a glimpse of him talking with a man who had just arrived. She tried to block thoughts of Grady from her mind, but without success.

Making her way through the quiet streets of Pinecrest, she grudgingly admitted that the man knew how to take charge and get things done. She should be glad that he was here. It would lighten her workload. But she worried that bad feelings concerning Nina might spill over into their work, even though he'd said it wouldn't.

Maria still wanted to set the record straight about Nina. Something told her the opportunity to tell her side of the story wouldn't come easily. She didn't want to force the issue.

For a moment this afternoon, Grady had been friendly, and she had forgotten how he had treated her at Nina's funeral. His belligerence then had shown his unforgiving spirit. So much about him reminded her of her father. Her father's workaholic nature had hurt her family. How many times had he promised to be at a sporting event, school play or birthday party, but not shown because something had come up at work? He'd left her heartbroken time after time. She'd seen the same thing in Nina's life with Grady.

But Maria couldn't hold that against him. No matter how he conducted his personal life, no matter how unforgiving he had been to her, God expected *her* to forgive. She had to remember not to be judgmental, but that was difficult to do where Grady Reynolds was concerned.

Chapter Two

Moving day. Clay and his family planned to move out this morning, and Grady would move in this afternoon. A tingle of anticipation and dread raced though Maria's mind at the thought of Grady and his girls occupying the downstairs apartment.

As she checked the Sloppy Joes warming in the Crock-Pot, she thought about her new home, under construction a few miles from town. Thankfully, it would be ready soon. Then she'd only have to deal with Grady's proximity at work.

Putting on an old gray T-shirt and well-worn jeans, Maria wondered what would happen when Grady and his girls arrived. Would Amanda and Kelsey remember her? How would they react to her after all this time? Had they wondered about her sudden absence from their lives after their mother died?

Maria shook the questions away as she tied her hair back in a ponytail and shoved her feet into the sneakers next to the door. Ready to join the moving crew, she grabbed a jacket before stepping outside. Although it was August, she shivered as the cool morning air raised goose bumps on her arms. Having grown up in California, she had forgotten that fall sometimes came early in this part of the country.

Jillian held up a steaming foam cup. "Hey, Maria, I've got coffee and doughnuts for you."

"Sounds good." Maria descended the stairs and squinted against the sun that shone brightly in a clear blue sky. When she took the cup from Jillian the hot liquid warmed her hands and took away the chill associated with living upstairs from Grady.

Maria took a bite of the doughnut and let the sugary sweetness melt in her mouth and ease her anxiety. She looked around. People from the church who had come to help with the move huddled near an SUV parked in front of the garage while they waited for the pickup trucks needed to move furniture.

Jillian grabbed Maria's arm and pulled her aside. "I haven't had a chance to talk to you. How's it really going with you and Grady?"

Maria wrinkled her brow. "What do you mean? Everything's fine."

"I just sensed a little tension when I met with you the other day."

"You noticed?"

"Yes, but I didn't want to say anything. What's going on?"

"Nothing that will affect our work."

"Is there some kind of problem I should know about?"

"It's personal."

"So I should mind my own business?"

Shrugging, Maria sighed. "It's just something from the past. It'll be okay."

"You're sure?"

"Yes." Maria hoped Jillian wouldn't press the issue. "Everything's fine, if you don't count all the problems we encountered with the final building inspection."

Jillian frowned. "Is everything resolved?"

"Yes. The plumbing in one area wasn't right. Grady was working with the inspectors and getting the subcontractors to come back and fix the problems. I've been working on the last-minute details for the opening, and we barely had time to talk before he left to get his girls. But he gave me a report. Everything's fixed. He took care of it all."

"That's great." Jillian took another sip of her coffee.

Maria couldn't deny Grady had a way of getting things done. He commanded respect and, she had to admit, she admired the way he moved things along. But she also remembered how he had used that commanding style to intimidate her after Nina's death. The past hung in her mind like the pesky mosquitoes that she swatted away in the morning air. As she finished off her doughnut, the trucks arrived. One of the church leaders handed out assignments to the workers.

Soon people were loading Clay and Beth's belongings onto the trucks. After most of the furniture was loaded, Maria and Jillian went inside to help Beth do some final cleaning.

"What have you heard from Grady?" Jillian asked Beth.

"He and the girls left yesterday afternoon and they spent the night just outside of Portland. They should get in about noon." Beth reached for a sponge and started cleaning the kitchen sink. "We should have everything ready for them to move in by then."

"Hey, Mom," Beth's son, Max, called as he sauntered into the kitchen, followed by four other teenage boys.

"Me and the guys have finished loading all the boxes. I'm going to drive them over to the new house."

Jillian leaned toward Maria and whispered, "Looks like Max has brought the front line from the football team."

"I'll have to have Max reserve these guys for my move."

"And when will that be?" Jillian asked.

Maria shrugged. "Before the snow comes, I hope. They told me ninety days after the basement was poured. That means just a few more weeks. I'm excited about having my own place."

"I know you're thrilled." Jillian touched Maria's arm. "But I still worry about you living out there in the woods all by yourself."

Maria chuckled. "No need to worry. There are three more houses going up on that road right now and land has been cleared for two more. I'll have neighbors before you know it."

The phone rang, and Beth grabbed it. When she finished talking, she turned to Maria and Jillian. "That was Grady. He's just heading out of Spokane. He'll be here in less than an hour."

"Great," Maria replied, although the thought of seeing Grady had her stomach in knots, for some reason. What was it? Dealing with the uncertainty of having him for a neighbor? Having to tiptoe around the past? She didn't want to think about it. "I'm going to head up to my apartment and get the food ready. Come on up when you're finished."

While Maria got out plastic plates, cups and utensils, she thought more about the reasons for her trepidation. Where had her early morning confidence concerning Grady gone? She wanted to live in harmony with Grady, but her tangled feelings about the situation made clear thinking difficult. She tried to pray. *Lord, I don't know how to deal with this situation. Please guide me.*

When the workers arrived back at the apartment, Maria served lunch, even though Grady hadn't gotten there yet. Soon the workers were occupying every available spot in Maria's small kitchen and living room and devouring Sloppy Joes. Everyone was laughing and talking—everyone except Maria, who could barely eat. The anticipation of Grady's arrival had taken away her appetite. She jumped when she heard loud footsteps on the stairs. Was that Grady? And why did it matter? She was acting as though they had some connection other than work. In a sense they did. The secret they shared, the secret of Nina's affair and subsequent death, bound them together in an unsettling way.

"Sounds like an invading army," Clay said with a chuckle as he went to the door.

When the door opened and Max and two of his football buddies entered, Maria released a long, slow breath. She hated the way she was feeling, but she didn't know how to overcome her crazy reaction to the thought of Grady's arrival.

"Hi, Mom," Max said, glancing in Beth's direction. "We unloaded the last truck. Two of the guys had to leave, but Drew and Nathan are going to hang out with me for a while." He sauntered into the kitchen. "Are we too late to eat?"

Maria handed each of the boys a plate. "No, help yourselves."

After the teens piled their plates high, Beth looked at Max. "Do you guys mind eating out on the front porch, so you can keep a lookout for the moving van?"

"No problem, Mom." Max headed for the door and he and his friends went down the stairs.

Ten minutes later, Maria turned at the sound of a knock. Clay opened the door.

"Well, we made it." Grady walked in, dressed in blue jeans and a green Oakland Athletics T-shirt. He was followed by his girls, who were also dressed in jeans.

Clay gave his brother a hug, then did the same to his nieces. "I'm so glad you're here. Do you want something to eat?"

Maria stood in the far corner of the kitchen and watched the family reunion. She had never seen Grady in such a casual and relaxed mode. Stubble covered his chin and his normally well-combed hair was disheveled, probably from the ball cap he had removed when he entered the room. She had the strange urge to hug him, too. She shook the ridiculous thought away and tried to concentrate on the girls.

Maria gazed at Amanda in amazement. Tall, with green eyes and auburn hair, the girl had an astonishing resemblance to her mother. And dressed in tight jeans and a formfitting top that showed off her well-developed figure, she didn't look thirteen. If Maria hadn't known better, she would have thought Amanda was seventeen or eighteen.

The teen remained silent as she gave her uncle and aunt a perfunctory hug. She had always been the quieter of the two girls, but Maria sensed that Amanda's silence now had more to do with not wanting to be there than with shyness.

Then Kelsey bopped into the kitchen, her light brown ponytail swinging behind her. When she saw Maria, she stopped in her tracks and stared.

Maria's heart melted as she read the question in Kelsey's blue eyes, so much like her father's. "Hi, Kelsey. I'm Maria. I used to stay with you sometimes. Do you remember me?"

"Maybe." Kelsey shrugged and wrinkled her nose as if she was searching her memory. "Did you read *Five Little Monkeys* to me?"

Nodding, Maria smiled. "Yeah, that was your favorite bedtime story."

"I still have that book."

"I'm glad you remember it. I always liked reading that one." Maria picked up a plate. "Let me get you something to eat."

As she fixed Kelsey's lunch, Grady moved into the kitchen. He placed his hand on Amanda's shoulder. "Amanda, say hi to Maria. You remember her, don't you?"

"I don't think so." Amanda's hair swished around her shoulders as shook her head. Her expression held no welcome.

Grady's nearness in the kitchen seemed to make the small space even smaller. Trying to push his presence from her mind, she took in Amanda's sullen face. Her look told Maria that even if the girl did remember, she didn't care. This was one unhappy teenager. Grady had his work cut out for him if he wanted to make his daughter happy about this move.

Grady and Kelsey joined the others in the living room, and the girl entertained the group by recounting their trip from California. Amanda took her plate and sulked in the corner of the kitchen. The two girls had always been different, but Maria now saw the differences between them as a wide schism.

After everyone had finished eating, Maria and Jillian

organized a cleanup detail. As Maria wiped the counter, loud footsteps sounded on the stairs again.

Breathless, Max burst into the room. "The van's here."

"Okay, tell them I'll be right down." Grady motioned to Amanda and Kelsey. "Come on, girls, you have to tell the movers where you want your stuff."

"Yippee." Kelsey jumped up and sprinted to the door.

Sporting a smile for the first time, Amanda eyed Max, her uncle's stepson, and his buddies as she sashayed across the room. "Sure, Dad."

Now *there* was trouble, if Maria had ever seen it. A thirteen-year-old who looked much older than her years and had a keen interest in boys. Maria didn't envy Grady the task of rearing that child.

Grady stood in the living room of his temporary home. Everything was in reasonable order—even Amanda and Kelsey's room. Kelsey had been eager to help, eager to please him, but Grady hadn't missed the fact that Amanda's cooperation came from her desire to impress Max and his friends. She had eagerly agreed to go with Clay and Beth for an ice-cream cone when she discovered that the teenage boys were also going. Even Kelsey's presence hadn't changed Amanda's mind. Grady was at a loss as how to deal with his older daughter. Sometimes he feared the worst.

Not wanting to think about Amanda, he flopped onto the brown tweed couch that sat against the front wall. Lacing his fingers behind his head, he stared at the dust motes swirling in the sunlight that beamed through the big picture window behind him. He let his mind dwell on the temporary nature of this situation. Half of his belongings would remain in storage until he found a permanent place. He'd start looking next week.

A knock on the back door startled him from his thoughts. He eased himself from the couch and strode toward the kitchen. When the back door came into view, he looked through the window in the upper half. Maria stood on the other side. She smiled and held up a coffeemaker.

He opened the door. "Come on in."

"You mentioned that you accidentally left your coffeemaker in storage. I have an extra you can use." She held it out.

"Thanks." When he took it, their fingers brushed. He steeled himself against the spark of reaction the contact created. He tried to tell himself it was nothing. An awkward silence filled the room. Grady wished she'd go away, but she made no move to leave. "Was there something else you wanted?"

"Yes. Jillian didn't get a chance to talk to you personally, so she asked me to invite you and the girls for supper on Monday night. Sam's going to do his barbecue."

"I'll be there, but the girls are going into Spokane to some concert on Monday night with Clay and Beth and a bunch of other kids."

"It's too bad Amanda and Kelsey will miss the barbecue, but they'll have other chances. These kinds of invitations are always in the works at JMR. Jillian treats her employees like a family."

"I gathered that from the way Clay talked."

"Amanda and Kelsey will have a great time with the church youth group."

Grady shrugged. "I suppose."

"I know you said you didn't want to discuss religion, but the church has a wonderful youth program. It might be a good place for Amanda and Kelsey to make some friends."

"No need for that. They'll make plenty of friends at school." He grimaced, knowing that Amanda was going to the concert only because Max and his friends would be there. Why had Maria mentioned the religion thing? Was this going to be something shoved in his face every time he turned around? As far as Grady was concerned, church wasn't a place where he could find peace. The church had let him down. If Nina hadn't gone to that Bible-study group, she would never have gotten involved with another man.

"It was just a thought," Maria said, without looking at him. "Anyway, Jillian suggested I give you a ride, since you haven't been out to their place."

"Fine with me."

She stared at him with those big brown eyes surrounded by long dark lashes. She glanced at the floor, then looked at him again and took a deep breath. "I know you said you didn't want to talk about the past, but I decided today that I can't live next door to you and work with you every day without discussing it. Whether you like it or not, we've got to clear the air."

Grady shook his head and rubbed the back of his neck. "I don't see the point."

"We just have to get it out of the way, once and for all. Then, we don't have to worry about stumbling onto the subject somewhere down the line."

He gritted his teeth, then forced himself to relax. "So what do you want to do?"

"I want to set the record straight about Nina. Will you listen?"

"What's there to say about a woman who ran off and left her husband and children to be with another man?" He narrowed his gaze. "A good wife and mother wouldn't do that."

"What she did doesn't mean she wasn't a good mother."

"In my opinion, it does."

"Well, maybe you were a…." Maria's voice trailed off.

"Maybe I was a what?"

"Nothing," she said, shaking her head. "I just wanted you to understand that no one's all good or all bad."

"So I'm just supposed to forget about what she did and pretend she was wonderful?"

Maria sighed. "I didn't say that."

"She ran off with another man, and you stood by and let her."

"That's not true." Maria's voice raised a pitch as she shook her head. "What should I have done? Left two little girls alone? I tried to talk Nina out of going with Carlos. I had no idea what she was planning until I got to the house. She told me she wanted me to stay with the girls for the weekend because she was going out of town and you were away on a case."

"You're telling me you had no idea my wife was having an affair with your cousin?" Realizing his question had come out as a shout, Grady took a deep breath to calm himself. In a lower voice, he said, "You were with her every week, when they were supposedly in Bible study together."

"They were. *We* were. We had a small group study. There were six or seven people on average. Sometimes after the study we'd go out for coffee. If you had ever bothered to attend yourself, you would have seen. We were all friends, sharing our problems and praying for one another."

"Plus other things." Grady couldn't keep the sarcasm out of his voice. "Seems like a lot of hypocrites, if you ask me."

"No, not hypocrites. Sometimes even Christians make bad choices. There are lots of examples—even in the Bible."

"I wouldn't know about that. I don't do much Bible reading. Except, I do know it says, 'Don't commit adultery.'"

"Yes, it does." Maria looked away and bowed her head.

The room grew eerily quiet. Was she praying? What was he supposed to say now? Had his grief made him judge her too harshly?

"Maria…" he said softly.

When she looked up, the sadness in her eyes was unmistakable. "I really didn't know what was going on. I thought they were just friends. As far as I knew the only time Carlos and Nina were ever alone together was the night her car wouldn't start. She called you, but you were involved in some meeting and couldn't come to get her. So Carlos offered her a ride."

"I was working."

"Did you ever think that might have been the problem? That you were always working?"

Grady didn't want to see her accusing expression. She seemed to think he was the one who had done wrong, not Nina. He walked to the other side of the room and rammed his hands into his pants pockets. He stared at the clock on the built-in oven. "You're blaming me?"

"No." Maria sighed. "What Nina did was wrong. I

was just pointing out the circumstances surrounding her decision."

Grady looked out the window over the sink. The darkening sky matched his guilt-ridden thoughts. He knew what Maria had said was true. Lawyers worked long hours. But Nina had known that when they'd gotten married. She'd promised "for better or for worse." What had happened to that vow?

He turned back to Maria. "You say Nina was wrong, but you still act as though it's my fault. Why?"

"The only thing I'm faulting you for is blaming *me* for something I didn't do."

Her accusation stung, but it was true. "I'm sorry. I was wrong. Can we start over?"

Smiling, she stepped toward the door. "Yes. I accept your apology. I'm glad we have that settled. We don't need to bring it up again."

"Yeah. Have a good night," he said, wondering whether they really did have it settled. A small doubt still lingered, leaving him uneasy as he watched her go.

She had forced him to face the past and get it out in the open. His grief over Nina's betrayal and her death, had made him push part of the blame on Maria. Could his apology really do away with the bad feelings about him she had harbored for the past four years? He'd been so mistaken. He could only hope his apology would erase the hurt of his wrongheaded accusations. Guilt still hovered in his mind. Guilt over the rash charges he had made against Maria and guilt over not being there for Nina.

Maria thought he'd been a lousy husband. She hadn't come right out and said it, but she'd hinted at it. And she was probably right. He wasn't good husband material. Maybe he and Nina had married too young. With the demands of law school, he'd been gone a lot even at the beginning of their marriage. He wouldn't make the mistake of going down that road again.

And yet, Maria had smiled when she accepted his apology. That smile had touched him deep down where all the guilt simmered. Her insistence on setting the record straight had freed him from some of his guilt. Oddly enough, despite his doubts and his self-reproach, relief was seeping into his psyche. For the first time since he'd come to Pinecrest, his heart was a little lighter.

Chapter Three

Grady stood next to Maria's car as she came out her front door. While she stopped to lock it, he studied the woman who had made him so terribly angry all those years ago, taking in her well-shaped figure dressed in jeans, a multicolored shirt and sneakers. She was a beautiful woman, even in her casual clothes, with her olive complexion and sable-colored hair brushing her shoulders in soft waves. And he had to admit an unexpected attraction to her.

Thinking of her in terms other than business was asking for all kinds of trouble. And even if they weren't working together, he didn't need another woman to complicate his life. Not that she would be interested, considering their unpleasant history.

She smiled as she came down the walk. It was the same forced smile he saw most of the time he was around her. He suspected she found it difficult to smile in his presence.

"Should I have worn jeans and sneakers?" He looked down at his khaki pants, red polo shirt and loafers.

"You'll be okay as long as Sam doesn't decide to take you on a hike through the woods." She went to the driver's side of the car and opened the door. "That's why I wore jeans. It's a bit rugged out on their property."

Shrugging, he looked at her over the top of the car. "Well, this will have to do. The only jeans I have are dirty. I wasn't expecting to go on a hike."

"I'm sure your clothes won't be a problem." She got into the car.

Grady got in, settled back and buckled his seat belt. He mulled over what they could talk about on this trip. Their day had been pleasant and productive. A good start to the week. He just hoped it would continue that way. He wanted a new beginning for his family. Would he find that here?

Neither of them spoke as they drove out of town. Wondering what this evening would bring, Grady glanced Maria's way. She appeared to be concentrating on the road. Maybe she preferred not to talk while she drove, but the silence was getting to him. Had they really put their bad history behind them? He hoped the past wouldn't interfere with their working relationship. He didn't want to talk about work, but what other safe topic of conversation was there? Watching the road ahead, he finally asked, "So how is it living in Pinecrest?"

"I'm getting used to living in a small town. Thankfully, if I have major shopping to do, Spokane isn't too far away."

Grady chuckled. "Women always think of shopping."

"Not always." Maria gave him a perturbed glance. "The best thing about Pinecrest is the people. They're wonderful, especially at the church I attend."

The church again. Did this woman talk about anything else? And it wasn't just her. Even Clay had been after him to come back to church. Well, he wasn't going to acknowledge what she'd said. "Good thing you like living in Pinecrest, since Jillian moved her foundation's headquarters here."

"So what do you think?" she asked, without looking his way. "It's a lot different than where you lived before."

"I figured if Clay liked it, I would, too. Besides, you know, we came from a small town. It just seems different, because California is more populated than this area."

"Do you have a Realtor?"

"No, Clay's going to hook me up with someone this week. He says we'll find housing prices much cheaper here." Grady wondered whether it bothered Maria to live near him. They had cleared up their misunderstanding, so he probably shouldn't worry. But he still had some concerns that his unkind treatment of her would continue to color their relationship. Could she really forgive and forget?

The interior of the car grew silent again as they sped down a road lined with hemlock, pine and spruce trees. He had to think of something else to say, so that his mind wouldn't be occupied with the woman sitting next to him. Max. Yeah, asking about Max would steer the topic in a new direction. Besides, maybe he could get an insight into the boy and his friends, who seemed to have captured Amanda's interest. Grady wasn't sure how to deal with his daughter's interest in boys. Amanda had him plenty perplexed.

"What can you tell me about Max?"

"Didn't you meet him at Clay and Beth's wedding?"

"Yeah, but what can you learn in a two-minute conversation? I know he's going to be a junior in high school and he plays on the football team. That's about it."

"As far as I can see, your nephew's just your average teenage boy. He's very active in the church youth group."

Grady groaned inwardly. More church talk. He should have expected that. He had surrounded himself with people whose lives centered on God, but he didn't want anything to do with God or people in the church. Their hypocrisy had stolen his wife from him and turned his life upside down. Ignoring Maria's reference to the church, he said, "I wonder how Clay will deal with his stepson."

"I guess you haven't seen them together."

"Only briefly."

"Max looks up to Clay. I think Max played a big part in getting Clay and Beth together."

Grady laughed. "Sometimes I have a hard time seeing Clay as a father figure. He definitely wasn't a role model in his younger days. He finally outgrew his wild streak, but I still think of him as my little brother."

"And you're not even taller than he is," Maria said with a chuckle. "I believe Clay is going to file papers to adopt Max as soon as they get settled in their new home."

"Yeah. He told me. My little brother is an extraordinary man."

"I have to agree." Maria gave him a sidelong glance. "I'm not sure how I would feel about taking on the lifelong responsibility of someone else's child."

"Well, I know he loves Beth enough to call her son his own."

"That's true. He loves Max, too."

"You're right." Grady wondered whether another woman could love his girls the way Clay loved Max. What did it matter? He wasn't planning to marry again. But sometimes he sensed that Amanda and Kelsey missed having a woman, a mother figure, in their lives.

Maybe Beth could help to fill that role. Could he possibly suggest that his new sister-in-law take the girls under her wing? Maybe it was something he should discuss with her when he got to know her better.

Turning off the highway, Maria glanced at him. "We're almost there. Just a couple miles up this road."

They fell silent as Grady took in the narrower road weaving its way through farmland surrounded by the nearby forest. The sun hovered in the western sky, just above the treetops on the distant hills. He hoped that being with Jillian and Sam would make conversation less difficult. Dealing with Maria in a business setting was easier than in a social one. Thankfully, he wouldn't have to see her socially very often.

Maria turned her car onto the steep drive leading to Jillian and Sam's house. As they crested the hill, he took in the two-story, cedar-sided house nestled in the pine forest. How would he survive this evening when he was surrounded by people whose lives were all about serving God? Ever since Nina's death, he had found it difficult to put his trust in God. He suddenly wished he were someplace else.

Maria parked in front of the five-car garage connected to the back of the house by a breezeway and deck. As she turned off the car, she looked his way. Was she wondering why he hadn't said a word since she had turned off the main road? Had she guessed that he wasn't overjoyed by this invitation? She was probably still at a loss as to why he had taken this job when everyone around him obviously made him uncomfortable.

"Well, we're here." She got out of the car.

Grady closed the car door and took a deep breath of

fresh country air filled with the scent of pine. He surveyed his surroundings and motioned toward the garage. "Do they have five cars?"

"Just two." Maria chuckled at Grady's reaction to the unusual garage. "They use the rest of it for a tractor, a van and equipment for the grounds."

He followed her up the front walk.

"Jillian tells me the place has changed a lot since she first saw it, a little over two years ago. The garage and deck weren't here and only the main floor of the house was finished." Maria stopped and looked at Grady before going up the steps to the porch. "Now they have two houses for children's home, plus an office and a barn for the horses. I'm sure you can get Sam to take you on a tour."

"Is that the hike you were talking about?"

Before Maria could answer the question, Jillian came through the front door. She carried a towheaded little boy who looked to be about a year old. "Come in, come in. Sam's out back tending to the barbecue."

Maria held out her arms. The little boy smiled and reached out to her immediately. She took him in her arms. "How's my little Sammy?"

The child giggled as Maria rubbed noses with him. A strange sensation swept over Grady as he watched the exchange. Tender feelings tugged at him. He wanted to believe they were for the child, but he couldn't deny that in the past few days, Maria had somehow shattered the guard he'd placed around his heart.

Jillian's voice interrupted Grady's thoughts. "I'll have to introduce you to Sam's pride and joy, Sam, Jr., better known as Sammy."

"Hi, Sammy." Grady stuck a finger out for the baby

to grab. Grady tried not to look at Maria as the little boy reached out with his chubby little hand and took hold.

"How are things at work?" Jillian asked, taking Grady's attention away from Maria and the baby.

"Good," he replied, thankful for Jillian's intrusion. Despite all his misgivings and all his mixed feelings about Maria, he knew that they had a good business relationship. The baby let go of Grady's finger, and he turned his attention to Jillian. "Maria and I had a very productive day. She's a great organizer." He glanced her way.

Maria stopped playing with the baby for a moment and gazed at him. He read the surprise in her expression before she looked at Jillian and said, "We did get a lot accomplished. We're all set for the grand opening three weeks from Saturday. We'll be working on budgets and orders for the rest of this week."

"I'm glad everything's falling into place," Jillian said as she led them into the house.

Grady surveyed the floor-to-ceiling stone fireplace as he followed the two women into the living room. He took a moment to admire the beamed ceiling before his gaze slid to Maria, who was bouncing the baby in her arms. He gurgled and laughed. Grady tried to look away, but the picture of Maria and Sammy against the backdrop of the homey room tugged at his mind again. Then Sam came through the door and rescued him.

Sam clapped him on the back. "Hey, Grady, glad you could come out."

Grady smiled as the aroma of barbecue wafted in through the French doors opening onto the deck. "Thanks. Food smells great. You need some help?"

"No, but come check out this built-in barbecue grill my parents gave me for my birthday a couple of years ago."

Maria continued to play with Sammy while she studied the two men, who both were about six feet tall, with lean muscular builds. They stood in front of a stainless steel barbecue that any chef would envy. Sam said something and Grady laughed. He appeared at ease, not uptight, as he had been with her on the ride out there.

"Are you and Grady working well together?"

"Didn't you ask me that once before?"

"Yeah, but I still see that tension. Why?"

Maria's mind spun. How should she answer that question? She bit her lower lip as she contemplated her response. She hated keeping things from Jillian, but she couldn't reveal the awful circumstances of Nina's death. Still, Jillian deserved some kind of explanation. "The problem is Nina's death. Nina and I were friends, and my presence just reminds Grady of a very painful time in his life."

"He's still hurting, isn't he?"

"Yeah."

"It's been four years. Seems like he should be moving on with his life by now." Jillian gave Maria a speculative glance. "Maybe you could help him with that."

Shaking her head, Maria laughed. "Not more of your matchmaking. You and Sam's sister, Kim, sure love to meddle in other people's lives."

Jillian gave her a look that was half grin and half grimace. "Sorry about that. We're just so happy that we'd like other people to find true love, too."

"I think I'm capable of doing that on my own."

"Yes, I'm sure you are, but a little help never hurts." Jillian held up her hands. "After all, when I moved back to Pinecrest, Kim gave Sam a little nudge in my direction. So I thought—"

"Forget that thought. It's a bad idea when we'll be working together."

"Well, if you change your mind, there *are* no company rules against it," Jillian said with an impish grin.

Maria bounced Sammy in her arms. "I won't change my mind."

"But don't you want one of these some day?" Jillian asked, rubbing Sammy's head.

"I can get my baby fix with this little guy anytime, then give him back. I spent enough time playing mom to my brother's kids." Maria sighed. "Maybe I'm selfish, but I feel like I deserve some 'me' time. So, please drop the subject."

"Consider it dropped." Jillian patted Maria's shoulder. "Anyway, I'm glad you and Grady are working well together."

"Yeah," Maria said, although she still wondered whether they had really put the past behind them. Hoping to make a change in the conversation, she asked, "Anything we can do to help Sam?"

Jillian shook her head. "Everything's ready. I'm just waiting on Sam to tell me when the meat's done. All I have to do is put things on the table."

"Let me help."

"You're already helping by taking Sammy."

"He's going to start walking any day now, isn't he?"

"I think so. Then I'll really have to watch him. He gets into enough trouble as it is."

Maria held Sammy out in front of her. "Are you giving your mom a hard time?" The little boy squirmed in Maria's arms. She set him down on the floor. He stood there for a moment and glanced around. "Jillian, look, I think he's going to take a step."

Jillian turned just as Sammy took two steps into Maria's waiting arms. "Oh, wow!" Jillian rushed to the deck. "Sam, you've got to come see this. Sammy just took his first steps!"

Sam dashed into the room. "Where?"

Jillian pointed. "Maria just stood him up, and he took two steps."

Sam hunkered down and held out his arms. "Come to Daddy, big boy."

Maria let go of Sammy's hands, and he staggered into his father's arms. Sam picked up his son and lifted him into the air. "That's my boy." Sam lowered the child and turned to Jillian. "Can't wait until he can play with Kim's boys."

Grady stood in the doorway. "Don't wish the time away."

"Yeah, I wasn't meaning to do that." Sam balanced his little boy in his arms. "I just got excited."

"It's an exciting time, but they grow up fast. Too fast sometimes." Although Grady's tone was congenial, Maria sensed regret, or maybe it was sorrow, in his statement. Had his girls grown up too fast after their mother died? Was he thinking about all the hours he had worked instead of spending time with his family?

Maria couldn't help remembering all the disappointments and tears of her own childhood. Over the years, she had come to understand why her father had worked so hard, but that still didn't take away the hurt. Was Grady realizing how his absence hurt his daughters?

"Sammy *is* growing up too fast," Jillian declared. "I can't believe he'll be a year old in just a few days. We're having a party. You're all invited."

Grady nodded. "Thanks."

"Let's get the meat off the barbecue before it burns." Sam handed the baby to Jillian and headed back to the deck.

Maria followed Grady as they helped carry food to the table. She vowed not to worry about Jillian's efforts to push Grady and her together. Jillian had no idea that Maria could never take an interest in a workaholic like Grady. They might be able to work together, but there was no way they could ever share anything remotely romantic.

Jillian set a basket of rolls on the table, then looked at Maria. "Hold Sammy while I get his high chair?"

"Sure." Maria reached for the baby, and he eagerly went into her arms.

While she held the little boy, he snuggled close, his little arms wrapped around her neck. As he pressed a wet kiss against her cheek, her heart warmed and sent her mind down a path she hadn't expected.

Despite her earlier declaration, maternal feelings slowly wound their way into her brain. She tried to push the thoughts away, but they burrowed deep down and wouldn't let go. Like Sammy clinging to her neck. She had meant it when she had said she wanted time for herself. But maybe at thirty her biological clock had started to tick louder than she realized.

Maria told herself there would still be plenty of time to get married and have children if the right man ever came along.

* * *

Steam curled into the air as Grady helped Sam get the barbecued ribs onto a big platter. The tantalizing smell of barbecue sauce mingled with the scent of the pine forest surrounding the house. Grady tried not to look at Maria, who was playing with Sam's little boy as she stood by the table. Something about her playing with that child pulled at his heart. He remembered how she had played with his girls when she visited Nina. Now he recognized that his girls had needed someone like Maria in their lives and he had pushed her away, because he'd thought Maria had betrayed them.

Jillian returned with the high chair and placed it at one end of the picnic table. Putting the baby in the chair, she surveyed the table. "Everything ready?"

"Looks that way. Find a place to sit, and we'll say a prayer." Sam took a seat next to Jillian, who had staked out her space at the end of the bench closest to the high chair.

Maria sat across from Jillian, and Grady had no choice except to sit next to Maria. At least this way he could avoid eye contact. Her presence was messing with his head. He didn't know what was bothering him. Attraction? Guilt? Remorse? Maybe all three. As he took his seat, the others joined hands.

Sam offered his hand to Grady across the table. "Our custom is to hold hands while we pray."

"Sure." Grady grasped Sam's hand, then held his other hand out to Maria. She placed her hand in his, and he quickly bowed his head. He didn't want her to look into his eyes and see that her touch had affected him. This was about prayer, nothing else. He tried to concentrate on what Sam was saying, but the only thing on Grady's mind was this woman, whose soft warm hand had him thinking about something other than God.

When the prayer was over, Jillian put a bib on Sammy and gave him a spoon that he immediately began banging on the high chair's tray.

"I think he's going to be a drummer." Sam gave his son a doting look. "Please give him something to eat, so we can have a little peace."

Jillian put a bowl of baby food on the tray and looked apologetically around the table. "Unfortunately, he likes to play before he lets me feed him."

"I'm not going to let a little noise keep me from enjoying this barbecue." Maria cut a rib from the rack on her plate. "You can't beat Sam's sauce. I keep telling him he needs to bottle it and sell it."

Jillian laughed. "Maria, always the entrepreneur and marketing genius, wants Sam to sell his sauce to help raise funds for the children's home."

"Just wait." Maria glanced around the table. "One of these days, I'm going to make Sam and his sauce as well known as Paul Newman."

Sam chuckled. "I'm not sure I want to be that famous."

Soon everyone was eating, laughing and talking. Grady began to relax as he and Sam talked about the upcoming football season. Although the women weren't involved in the men's discussion, Maria's voice and gentle laughter somehow filtered into Grady's mind. He tried harder to concentrate on his conversation with Sam, but nothing seemed to obliterate her presence beside him.

After they finished the meal, they all pitched in to clear the table and clean up. While they worked, Grady realized he had found more enjoyment in the evening than he'd expected. He liked Jillian and Sam. That was one of the reasons he'd taken this job. Then there was the chance to reconnect with his little brother after their years apart. Despite all these good things, he still didn't know how to act around Maria. Even though he had been wrong about her part in Nina's betrayal, her presence always reminded him of it. How was he going to deal with that? He kept asking himself that question.

"Hey, Grady, how about a tour of our place?" Sam's question penetrated the fog of Grady's thoughts.

"Sure," Grady replied, then glanced at Maria with a wry smile. "I was told I might have to do a little hiking."

"Well, we won't do any strenuous hiking. We'll keep to the beaten paths around here. Sometime, I'll take you on a hike up and down our mountain."

"You have a mountain to climb?"

"Well, it's not exactly a mountain, more like a hill, but a steep one. The climb will definitely get your heart rate going. Just like our lake is more of a pond. But we like to pretend everything is big." Sam chuckled. "Are you ladies coming with us?"

"Sure," Jillian replied before Maria could make her wishes known. "Let me get Sammy's backpack."

As Jillian disappeared into the house, Grady wondered whether Maria was as interested in the hike as Jillian, or if she was just playing the polite guest? In a moment, Jillian returned with the carrier. Sam slipped it on, and she deposited Sammy in it. The baby gurgled and patted Sam's head as they left the deck.

Leading the group, Sam started down a blacktop road that wound its way through the ponderosa pines. They came to a single-story, cedar-sided house tucked among the towering trees and another one just yards down the road. "These are our two residential homes. Eight children and their houseparents live in each one."

"Have the children here lost their parents?" Grady asked, thinking about his own girls.

Sam shook his head. "Most of the kids are from abusive homes or have substance abuse or behavioral problems. The kids come to us through church and family recommendations. We provide counseling for the children and parents. We try to reunite families, but sometimes that doesn't work. In those cases, the children continue to live here."

While Sam talked, Grady couldn't help thinking about his own parenting problems. If he asked for help, would they push religion at him? He couldn't picture the church helping, when the church had been the cause of his difficulties in the first place. Trying to take his mind off his own troubles, Grady asked, "Do the kids attend the local schools?"

"Yeah, since I'm going into school each day, we transport them in our big van. On Sundays we use the van and cars to take everyone to church." Sam stopped along the road and pointed to the land that had been cleared. "We're planning two more residences. Over Labor Day, we're having a big campout and work weekend. Folks from our congregation and several churches from Spokane are coming out to frame the houses and get them under roof before the colder weather hits. I hope you'll join us."

Maria came to stand beside Grady on the road. "Your girls would love getting to know some of the other kids better and they'd have fun helping."

What could he say? Was Maria trying to make it impossible for him to refuse? He would sound uncharitable if he didn't agree to come. But he didn't want to give the wrong impression about his intentions as far as church was concerned. "Sounds like a good cause. We'll see. We have a lot of settling in to do."

"I'm sure you do—" Jillian patted his arm "—but we'll be there to help you."

"Thanks," Grady said, resigning himself.

Sam continued the tour by taking them to the barn and corral. The smell of hay and animals greeted them as they entered the barn. A horse nickered. A couple of cats scurried across their path.

"We have a dozen horses here. The older kids learn to ride and they have to care for the horses. Each child has chores and responsibilities," Sam explained.

Grady studied the pictures of children that hung on one wall of the barn. They smiled while they groomed the horses. "You have a wonderful operation here."

"Thanks. We hope it will make a difference in the lives of these kids." Sam motioned toward the door. "Let's head back."

No one spoke as they retraced their steps along the road toward the house. The peaceful quietness of the forest seemed to reach out and touch Grady's soul. This was the kind of peace he wanted in his life—a peace where he could forget the hurts of the past. Could he find what he was looking for here in this quiet place, away from the noise of his former life? He wanted to believe he could.

As they rode back to town, shades of pink and orange from the setting sun painted the sky. The tall pines at the edges of the fields of grain appeared black against the colorful backdrop. Grady wished that somehow the beauty of the scenery could take away his unsettled feelings. The visit to the children's home had made him think about his relationship with his daughters, especially Amanda. She was a troubled child, and he wasn't sure how to deal with her problems. After listening to Sam talk about the kids they were helping, Grady knew his daughter needed more guidance than he could give her.

"You're awfully quiet." Maria's statement momentarily turned his thoughts away from his problems.

"Just thinking about the children's home." Looking at Maria reminded him of another problem. How was he going to deal with her? Tonight he couldn't help noticing the genuine affection between Maria and Jillian. Was that the kind of friendship Maria had had with Nina? He hadn't been around enough to know. Guilt gnawed at him again.

"Sam and Jillian have a real passion for helping others. I'm so glad to be a part of their ministries." Maria gave him a speculative glance as she stopped the car at the stop sign. "You know, it will involve a lot of church activities. Like the house raising."

Grady's stomach knotted. "Yeah. Jillian knows how I feel about church, but she still hired me."

"Well, don't be surprised if you find yourself more involved in church activities than you'd ever planned." Maria turned the car onto the main highway. "Have you ever talked with Beth about her experiences?"

Grady shook his head. "No, I haven't had the opportunity to get to know her very well. Our meetings have been short and filled with lots of other people. That's one of the reasons I took this job. I wanted to be closer to Clay and Beth."

"Then you'll find God front and center in their lives."

Grady knew that was true, but he had hoped somehow it wouldn't affect him. Now he figured he had been kidding himself. "I am, but Clay knows how I feel. Everyone does, including you."

Maria said nothing in response, and Grady's thoughts returned to Amanda's problem. He hadn't shared his worries with anyone. He didn't know where to turn. Nothing had been right since Nina's death. How could he disclose his utter shock at finding a nearly empty bottle of vodka in Amanda's closet? How could he determine whether she was telling the truth about it? Her belligerent attitude colored every aspect of her life. She was only thirteen years old, and he feared she was headed for major trouble. How could he help her?

Maybe this move would get her away from wrong influences. The discovery of the bottle had prompted him to reexamine his own life. Something drastic had to be done. Yet he wondered whether the move would just put more problems in his lap.

Darkness descended around them as they neared Pinecrest. The streetlights glowed in the dusk. Everything about the quiet little town made him feel he could find the answers he sought. Was he basing his hopes on a false premise? Would he find more problems than answers? Maria's presence raised those questions. He had to quit worrying about her. He had enough worries that didn't involve her.

When they reached their street, Maria drove down the alley and parked her car in the garage. As she opened her door, the dome light lit the car's interior. She looked at him. "You can park your car in here if you want. There's plenty of room. Then you won't have to park on the street."

"Yeah, I'll do that."

They strolled silently along the walk leading to the back of the house. Maria stopped at the stairway that led to her upstairs apartment. "I'll see you in the morning."

"Sure. Good night." Grady watched her climb the stairs and disappear into her apartment.

After her door clicked shut, the light next to the door went off. He stood on the wraparound porch in the darkness and gazed at the sky. Away from the bright city lights, the stars sparkled against the blackness. Was there a God up there who had placed the stars and moon in the heavens, or was that story a fairy tale? He had once put his trust in God, but that trust had come unglued with Nina's betrayal.

"If You're up there, God, why did You allow that to happen?" he whispered.

Silence greeted him.

With a heavy heart, he sighed and unlocked the door to his temporary home. He went inside and flopped on the couch. He sat alone in the dark and hoped he had made the right decision to uproot his girls and move here. Nina's death had devastated them all. Amanda hid her hurt behind belligerence, Kelsey behind her happy face and he behind his work. Could being here, away from constant reminders of Nina in California, get rid of their pain? But here, one reminder still remained.

Maria.

Chapter Four

Carrying a blue gift bag with blue-and-white checkered tissue paper sticking out of the top, Maria hurried down the stairs and along the porch. She stopped short outside Grady's back door when she heard Amanda's raised voice.

"I don't care what you say. I'm not going to some dumb birthday party for a one-year-old." Not even the closed door could blunt her defiant tone.

Wondering what she should do, Maria stood glued to the spot. She didn't miss Grady's responding angry tones. "You're treading on dangerous territory, young lady. You *will* be going."

"Why should I have to go to a birthday party for a one-year-old? It'll be so lame."

"Max will be there. If he can go, so can you."

"He'll just make a boring party more boring."

Maria puzzled over that statement. Amanda had seemed enthralled with Max and his friends on moving day. Was she just being obstinate to irritate her father?

"Boring or not, you're going, or you'll be grounded." Grady's loud response shook Maria from her thoughts.

"Who cares? There's nothing to do around this dumb town, anyway."

The door opened and Amanda raced onto the porch, nearly bumping into Maria. Amanda's green eyes opened wide. "What're you doing here?"

Before Maria could answer, Grady stepped out the door. Looking at Maria over the top of Amanda's head, he grimaced, looking embarrassed, as if he knew she had heard their conversation. Then he looked at his daughter. "That's no way to talk to Maria. I asked her to ride with us out to the Lawsons' place, so we don't get lost."

Narrowing her gaze, Amanda pouted while she glanced from Maria to her father. "Might as well get lost."

"I don't want to hear another word." Grady gritted his teeth and pointed toward the garage. "Go to the car."

Amanda glared at him. Mumbling something under her breath, she shuffled across the porch and down the steps into the backyard.

Grady turned and poked his head back through the door. "Kelsey, hurry up. Bring the gift. We're ready to leave."

In a moment Kelsey, smiling brightly, appeared at the kitchen door. She held up a red gift bag decorated with blue, green and yellow balloons. "I'm ready, Dad. Here's the gift."

"Good. You can carry it." He glanced at Maria. "Let's go."

Swinging the bag, Kelsey skipped across the yard toward the garage while Grady and Maria followed. Kelsey exuded energy and a zest for life. Her happiness was almost infectious.

Grady glanced at Maria as Kelsey got into the backseat with Amanda. "They're like night and day. Sorry about Amanda. She's not making this move easy."

Maria gave him a wry smile. "Teenage girls can be very moody."

"Is that the problem?" He laughed halfheartedly.

Maria shrugged. "Maybe. I was just comparing my experiences with my oldest brother's teenage daughter. I noticed she had some of the same attitudes."

"When does it get better?"

"I think it all depends on the kid."

"That doesn't tell me much."

"Maybe you ought to talk to Sam. He's the one who deals with teenagers. Me, I'm more into the geriatric crowd."

Grady chuckled. "You and me both."

"I'm looking forward to tonight. What about you?"

"I'm just hoping we get through the evening without Amanda causing a scene. I'll be relieved if she behaves and doesn't spend the whole evening pouting and letting everyone know she doesn't want to be there."

Maria didn't know what else she could say. Maybe a little prayer was called for. *Lord, please give Grady the help he needs to deal with Amanda. And help him to see Your love through me.*

With the prayer floating through her thoughts, she joined Grady in the front seat. Glancing at her sideways, he buckled his seat belt and turned the key in the ignition. Maria's heart beat a little faster, and her stomach did one of those flip-flops that unsettled her. Why was she letting this guy get to her? He was the last man in whom she should have an interest, with his workaholic past and troubled daughter. She finally had time for herself. She couldn't let anything derail that.

As Grady drove out of the alley onto the street, Maria glanced in the back. "Are you girls eager for school to start?"

Amanda scowled and rummaged in the backpack she had sitting on her lap as she ignored Maria's question.

Despite her seat belt, Kelsey managed to bounce in her seat. Just watching her made Maria tired. "Yeah. I met my teacher today when we went to school to register. She's really nice. Aunt Beth introduced me. We've been helping Aunt Beth make stuff for her classroom. That's cool. I like it."

"That's great. Your aunt Beth told me they have a really fun fall festival at your school every year."

"I know. She said I could help her bake something for the bake sale. Dad doesn't do much baking."

"Hey, I make great pancakes."

Kelsey laughed. "You can't sell pancakes at a bake sale."

Maria took in the playful kidding between father and daughter. She had never seen that side of Grady, even when she had been a friend of Nina's. He had always been in a hurry to be in court or at some meeting. But most of the time he hadn't been home at all.

Maria glanced at Amanda again. She had donned a pair of earphones and bobbed her head to the music on the iPod she'd dug out of her backpack. She had retreated into her own little world. Maria tried to think back to her teenage years. Had she been moody and seemingly self-absorbed as Amanda? Probably not. Her brothers wouldn't have allowed it.

A question from Kelsey interrupted her thoughts. "Hey, Dad. Do you think we'll get to ride the horses?"

"I don't know, Kels. But if we don't get to ride tonight, we'll make arrangements to do it some other time. Okay?"

"Cool." Kelsey tapped Maria on the shoulder. "Maria, do you know how to ride a horse?"

Turning to look at Kelsey, Maria nodded. "I used to ride a lot, but I've been really busy lately. Sometimes I help Sam out when they have trail rides."

"I can hardly wait. I think it'll be fun."

"Now, Kels, don't get your heart set on riding horses tonight. This is Sammy's birthday party. This isn't about you getting to ride horses."

"I know, Dad, but I can hope, can't I?"

"Yeah. You can hope."

For the remainder of the drive, Kelsey chattered, filling the otherwise silent car with her opinions on numerous topics. For an eight-year-old child, she was a fountain of information and she loved to share everything she knew.

"Where do you learn all this stuff?" Maria asked.

"On the Internet, but we don't have Internet service here yet."

Maria figured that was a good thing. She speculated about the wisdom of letting a little girl surf the Internet at will. Did Grady monitor what his daughter did while she was on her computer? It wasn't any of her business, but she worried that he didn't keep an eye on Kelsey as he should. After all, as far as Maria could tell, he had been mostly an absentee father. But she needed to remind herself that this wasn't her concern. She didn't have the right to tell him how to deal with his kids.

Grady pulled to a stop in the drive behind several other cars. As he got out, voices and laughter coming from the back of the Lawsons' house floated his way. People gathered on the deck and spilled into the yard surrounded by the nearby forest. Kelsey grabbed Maria's hand and dragged her across the gravel drive. Laughing, Maria joined her in a sprint, their gift bags swinging as they raced toward the house.

Taking a deep breath of the pine-scented air, Grady hoped the evening would go well. He tried to ignore the way the scene between Maria and Kelsey touched something deep inside him where he had buried his feelings for a long, long time. Feelings that hadn't stirred since Nina's death.

Would Kelsey's obvious attachment to Maria be a problem in the future? Kelsey had often mentioned how much she wanted a mother and, although Amanda seemed indifferent about the topic, he suspected she felt the same. But he couldn't bring himself to think about marrying again. He just wasn't good husband material. He needed to concentrate on being a good father.

He took in the forest and the nearby hills, in hopes that the beautiful scenery could bring peace to his jumbled thoughts, but any peace was short-lived. He looked at Amanda. Still sporting the earphones, she was dragging her feet as though she were headed to a death sentence rather than a party.

Grady had a similar feeling—one of being trapped between trying to please his new boss and having to deal with a daughter who might ruin the evening with her attitude. He'd been tempted to leave her at home but had feared that option, as well. Could he trust his daughter not to get into some kind of trouble? He wasn't worried so much during the day, when he was close by at work, but being fifteen miles out of town at night was another matter. Somehow he had to resolve this problem. Was talking with Sam the answer?

No, that wasn't the answer. He couldn't make a new start here by opening up his life and problems to others. He had to forget all that stuff and just deal with tonight. As he approached the deck, Maria and Kelsey greeted Jillian and handed her the gift bags. Sammy clung to Jillian's leg. The little boy seemed overwhelmed by all the people, unlike the other evening, when Maria and he had been the only guests.

Kelsey bent down and made a funny face at Sammy. He laughed. She held out her arms, and he toddled toward her. She gathered him into a hug, and Maria helped her take him over to the built-in bench on the deck. Kelsey had worked her charm on the shy birthday boy.

"What am I supposed to do?" Amanda's sulky question made Grady turn his attention away from Maria and Kelsey.

He eyed Amanda. Her pout matched her inquiry. "You could come with me and say hello to Jillian and little Sammy."

"I'll pass."

"Suit yourself." He headed for the deck before he could say or do something to make her more unreasonable.

He didn't know how to respond to her moodiness. Sometimes he just wanted to shake her and tell her to grow up and realize she had a pretty good life compared to a lot of other kids. But he had to remember losing a mother was hard for a young girl. How could he fault her when he had issues of his own about losing a wife? He hadn't been there to comfort his girls when they needed him. Guilt ate at him whenever he thought about how, buried in his own grief, he had abandoned them emotionally. He had to make it up to them somehow. But what would it take?

Just as he reached the steps going up to the deck, he glanced back. With the pout still marring her pretty face, Amanda was leaning against a tall pine at the edge of the yard. He didn't have time to deal with her attitude now. He had to join in the festivities whether she did or not.

"Hey, Grady." Sam's voice made him turn.

"Sam." Grady shook Sam's hand. "Looks like the party's in full swing."

"Yeah. Almost everyone is here. We're still waiting on Jillian's parents."

"How's her mom doing?"

"For the most part, she's doing well. She has some bad days, but most of the time things are good. They're coming later so she doesn't get worn-out. If she gets too tired, she could have a bad night. Makes it hard on Jillian's dad."

"How is Jillian taking it all? She sounded so upbeat when she convinced me to take the job here. I had no idea her mother suffered from Alzheimer's until Clay told me."

"Jillian doesn't like to talk about it much."

"I'm sure that's hard."

Sam nodded. "She likes to look on the positive side. Her mother still knows her family. That's the important thing in Jillian's mind. And she knows when the time comes there'll be a top-notch facility to care for her mother's needs. In the meantime, the facility will help other families cope with relatives who need long-term care."

"It's good to be a part of that."

"We're glad you are, too." Sam clipped Grady on the back, then turned at the sound of a car in the drive. "Looks like Jillian's folks are here. The party can begin."

While Sam went to greet his in-laws, Grady made his way onto the porch, where he said hello to Jillian. She introduced him to her siblings, their families and the two sets of houseparents for the children's home. As he met the various members of her family, he noticed that one of her nieces looked to be about Amanda's age. Could he somehow get the two girls together?

After Jillian finished the introductions, she glanced around. "I see Kelsey here, but where's Amanda?"

Grady nodded toward the edge of the yard. "She's standing over there, listening to her music."

"Oh, yeah, I see her. She seems to be the shy one."

"I suppose you could say that."

Kelsey jumped up from the bench where she had been playing with Sammy. "Amanda's not shy. She just didn't want to come because she thought she couldn't have any fun at a birthday party for a little kid."

Heat crept up Grady's neck. Leave it to Kelsey to lay the truth on the line. "Kelsey—"

Kelsey interrupted him. "Well, it's true, Dad."

"Yes, but—"

"That's okay, Grady." Jillian patted him on the arm. "I can understand why she wouldn't be thrilled about going to a birthday party for a one-year-old."

"No, it's not okay."

"Don't worry about it. I'm not. And Sammy certainly doesn't care." Jillian chuckled and summoned her niece with a wave of her hand. "Lauren, why don't you say hi to Amanda? She's standing over there at the edge of the yard."

Although the girl tried to smile, Grady couldn't mistake the grimace that crossed her face as soon as Amanda's name was mentioned. Amanda had probably already made her displeasure at being in Pinecrest well known. "Sure, Aunt Jillian."

Kelsey joined Lauren as she stepped off the deck. "I'll go, too."

A relieved smile brightened Lauren's face. "Okay."

Grady wondered what could have happened to make Lauren so reluctant to be with Amanda. Would Clay know? Grady scanned the yard for his brother and finally saw him standing off to one side of the yard. Grady made his way in that direction. Before he got there, a young man who held a little girl in his arms approached and started a conversation with Clay. Grady frowned. Now he wouldn't be alone with Clay and have a chance to ask him about Amanda.

"Hey, Clay. Are you guys getting settled in the new house?" Grady asked.

Clay nodded. "We're making progress." He glanced at the young man beside him. "Have you met Dylan, Jillian's nephew?"

"Yeah, Jillian introduced us earlier."

"But you didn't meet the apple of my eye." Dylan glanced down at the little girl. "This is my daughter, Emma."

"Hi, Emma." Grady remembered when his girls had been that age. It had been so much easier then.

Before anyone could say another word, Sam rang a cowbell. It sounded through the yard and the woods beyond. Everyone stopped talking and turned their attention toward the deck. Holding the birthday boy, Sam stood at the railing. "Thanks, everyone, for coming to share this day with us. We'll have a word of thanks, then you can proceed through the line starting at the far end of the deck."

Grady watched while the others bowed their heads for the prayer. Sometimes he wanted to pray for help, but God never seemed to be there. And despite the love and acceptance of these people who proclaimed the goodness of God, Grady was afraid to trust them. They always did something to disappoint, and Grady was tired of disappointments. He barely listened as Sam spoke a prayer of thanksgiving for the food. Grady didn't want to be sucked into their world, only to be let down.

The night air was filled with laughter and conversation. The partygoers ate, sang "Happy Birthday" and had a good laugh as Sammy made a mess with his piece of birthday cake. After everyone had cake, Sam and Jillian helped Sammy open his presents. Everyone got a chuckle out of Sammy's fascination with the gift bags and the wrapping paper. Grady couldn't help thinking about happier times with Amanda and Kelsey. When he glanced Amanda's way, he found her still looking glum.

Throughout the evening, Grady looked for an opportunity to talk to Clay, but he was constantly in conversation with someone. While he waited for a chance to talk with Clay, Grady kept an eye on Amanda. She had eaten at one of the picnic tables with the other kids, but she never seemed to join in their conversations. When the others played in a volleyball game, she continued to sit at the table and listen to her music. He was tempted to go over and rip the earphones out of her ears and take her iPod away. But that certainly wouldn't make things any better. What was going through that child's mind? Maybe he didn't want to know.

He decided to put his focus elsewhere and moseyed over to watch the kids play volleyball. Even Kelsey had joined one of the teams, which were made up of kids of all ages. While he stood there, Clay and Beth joined him.

"Who's winning?" Clay asked.

"Max's team." Grady figured this was his chance to talk to Clay, even though Beth was there. Maybe she could shed some light on Amanda, too. "You have a minute to talk?"

Clay turned his attention away from the game. "About what?"

"Amanda."

"What about her?" Clay glanced around. "Where is she?"

Grady tilted his head. "Don't look there now, but she's leaning up against a tree at the back of the yard."

"So why would I know about Amanda?" Clay asked, slowly turning his head. "Okay. I see her. She's still absorbed in her music."

"She's been that way since we left home. I've just let her be, because I didn't want to make a scene, but I haven't been happy with her behavior."

"She hasn't been any trouble, as far as I can see," Clay said with a puzzled frown.

"It's her attitude." Grady shook his head. "She didn't want to come, so she's been pouting all night."

"So what can I tell you?"

"How was she the night you took the kids to that concert?"

Clay didn't say anything right away. He just stared for a moment, then turned to look at Beth. She looked back at him and shrugged her shoulders.

Grady recognized the silent communication for what it was—a reluctance to answer his question. "Okay. What are you guys not telling me? What happened that night?"

"What makes you think something happened?"

"Well, when we first got here, Jillian asked her niece to talk to Amanda. I sensed the girl's hesitation. And Amanda has kept to herself all night. Even if she didn't want to be here, that's just not like her. So tell me what's going on."

"I don't know, Grady," Clay said. "I'm not sure you want to hear about it."

"Absolutely, I want to hear. If Amanda did something, I should know about it."

"It's not that simple."

Grady looked at Beth. "Is it that bad?"

She shrugged. "It's not just about Amanda. I don't want you to be angry with Max."

Grady frowned. "What does Max have to do with it?"

"How's the volleyball game going?" Maria's voice sounded behind them. "Looks like they're having fun."

"Yeah," Grady replied, his heart sinking. His chance to get the information he wanted from Clay was gone. He couldn't talk about this in front of Maria. It was bad enough that he had to discuss the problem with his little brother.

"I just wanted to let you know that we can leave whenever you'd like. Just tell me." Maria turned to leave. "I'll be up on the deck."

"Maria, you can't leave." Beth reached out and grabbed Maria's arm. "We've hardly talked since we've moved."

Maria stopped. "I know."

"We'll have to have you out to the house for dinner sometime," Beth said.

Grady took in the women's conversation with growing irritation. He suspected Beth had waylaid Maria on purpose in order to keep from answering his question.

Well, he wasn't going to let that happen. "Clay, the women can talk while we take a walk down by the lake."

His brother gave him a knowing smile. "Sure."

The two of them walked across the lawn to the woods surrounding the small lake at the bottom of the hill. "Please tell me about Amanda. I should know what's going on with her. I'm her father."

Clay sighed. "I know, but Beth was afraid you'd be angry with Max. That's why she didn't want to get into it."

"So is this a problem with Max or a problem with Amanda?"

"Both."

"Just tell me."

Clay sighed again. "Okay. On the way to the concert, Amanda was flirting unmercifully with a couple of Max's friends. She made sure she sat by the guys during the concert."

"Did that upset Max?"

"Just let me finish."

Nodding his head, Grady grimaced. "Okay."

"Anyway, we stopped for ice cream on the way home. When we got back into the van, Amanda tried to sit with those guys again. Max pulled her aside and told her she was coming on too strong with the guys. I think he was trying to give her some friendly advice, but she took it the wrong way."

"So what did she do?"

"She kind of went off on Max, saying they were all a bunch of hicks. That Pinecrest was a lame town. That she wished she'd never moved here."

"No wonder Jillian's niece didn't want to talk to Amanda."

"Well, Max could have handled it in a better way. He could have waited until later to talk to her. Calling her out in front of everyone just embarrassed her. He should've known better."

"Clay, you don't have to make excuses for her. I know Amanda has some problems. I'm just not sure how to handle them."

"Talk to Sam."

"That's what Maria said, too."

"You discussed this with Maria?"

"Not exactly. Amanda and I had an argument before we came tonight and Maria just happened to hear it. That's all."

"Well, I think talking to Sam would help."

"Is he going to spout a bunch of church stuff to me?"

Clay shrugged. "I don't know, but it wouldn't hurt for you to put God back into your life. Maybe that's what Amanda needs."

"I doubt it." Grady shook his head. "She doesn't need a bunch of people preaching at her and then turning around and doing just the opposite of what they preach."

"Is that the way you view the church?"

"Yes."

"Why? Does this have anything to do with Nina's death? Do you blame God for that?"

Grady looked toward the lake ahead of them. How could he answer that question? It hung there like one of the tree branches along the trail to the lake. Just as the way ahead of them was strewn with rocks and fallen trees, Grady's lost connection with God was strewn with the wreckage of his marriage and the trouble with his children. "I don't know—"

"I don't intend to make any judgments," Clay interrupted. "I just want to understand."

"How can you understand, when I'm not sure I understand myself?"

Clay didn't respond. They finished their walk to the lake, made their way to the dock and walked to the end. The water lapped along the shore. Frogs croaked in the waning light. As the sun sank behind the trees lining the shore, the full moon glowed just above the treetops. Grady sensed in Clay a reluctance to speak, as though saying something would disturb the beauty of the setting. At times like this, it was almost possible to believe that a God had set all this in motion. But when he looked at his life, he saw no evidence of God.

Finally, Clay laid his hand on his shoulder. "Grady, I'm worried about you."

"Because of Amanda?"

"No, because you've turned away from God."

"I don't see any point in discussing this."

"There is a point. The salvation of your soul."

Grady turned to leave. "Save your preaching for someone else."

Clay ran ahead and blocked the path. "I'm sorry. I didn't mean to preach. I just know how much my faith in God has helped my life." Surveying the lake, Clay waved his hand in the air. "Look at the wonders of creation. God's power is evident everywhere."

Grady stared past Clay, and wondered how to respond. Maria's voice echoed through the forest. "Grady, come quick!"

He raced off the dock to meet her. "What's happened?"

She hurried along the trail until they met halfway up the hill. "Kelsey's been hurt."

"Hurt how?" Grady's heart pounded as it jumped into his throat.

"In the volleyball game—" Maria paused to catch her breath. "She collided with one of the other kids and fell. She might have broken her arm."

Chapter Five

Maria didn't have time to say anything else before Grady sprinted up the hill. She raced to catch up to him, but his long legs covered the ground much faster than hers. When she finally reached the backyard, Grady was already up on the deck, hunkered down beside a tearful Kelsey. Someone had put ice in a bag and she was holding it on her lower arm. Maria hurried onto the deck.

"What do you think?" Grady asked, glancing up at Sam.

"Only a doctor can tell for sure whether it's broken," Sam replied, his expression painted with concern. "I think you should take her to the emergency room."

Grady stood. "Where's Maria?"

"Right here." She stepped forward. "I'll drive you to the hospital."

Grady helped Kelsey to the car. Even Amanda hurried along, losing her pout as she got in the front seat. Grady helped Kelsey into the back.

"We'll say a prayer," Sam called as they drove away.

* * *

Silence filled the car as they sped toward Pinecrest. No one seemed eager to talk. When they reached the hospital, Maria pulled into the emergency-room drive. Grady helped Kelsey out of the car, and Amanda hopped out and joined them.

Maria leaned across the seat and called after her. "Amanda, tell your dad I'll be in as soon as I park the car."

She nodded and hurried after them.

When Maria entered the waiting area outside the emergency room, her sneakers squeaked on the light gray tiled floor. The smell of antiseptic permeated the air. A young couple and an older woman sat on the blue vinyl-covered chairs that lined one wall of the room. A TV perched on a stand high in the corner of the room broadcast a sitcom. The laugh track belied the concern on the faces of the people seated there.

Maria spied Amanda sitting on the edge of one of the chairs. She was twisting her hands in her lap as she stared at the double doors on the other side of the room. Maria didn't miss the worry in Amanda's eyes.

"Kelsey'll be okay," Maria said, sitting next to Amanda.

Amanda released a heavy sigh. "I know, but I hate hospitals. They remind me of when my mom died."

"I'm sorry I wasn't around much after that happened."

Hoping the girl would accept some comfort, Maria laid a hand on Amanda's arm. She appeared more her age now. Her concern for her sister took away the aloof air she had managed to produce most of the evening. For once, she wasn't trying to act older.

She looked at Maria. "It wasn't your fault. Dad pushed everyone away."

Maria marveled that Amanda, even as a nine-year-old grieving over the loss of her mother, could have realized what her father had done when his wife died. Maria wondered whether Amanda had any idea what had been happening with her mother. Probably not. Maria hadn't even known that her good friend was having an affair.

"Would you like to say a little prayer for Kelsey?" Maria asked.

Amanda nodded. "Okay."

Relieved and a little surprised at Amanda's response, Maria held out a hand. While they held hands and bowed their heads, Maria gave a short prayer for Kelsey. When Maria finished, she glanced at Amanda. Her eyes welled with tears. She blinked them away as she straightened her shoulders and pressed her back into the chair. She stared straight ahead.

Maria wished she knew what to say to the girl to make things better. She tried to think back to her own teen years. Her life had been very different. Maria'd had no sisters. Only brothers. She came from a large family and her parents were both still alive. How could she relate to a motherless child?

"Do you ever think about my mom?" Amanda's question startled Maria.

"Yes, I do." Maria speculated about what had prompted the question. "When I first saw you, the day you moved in, I thought about how much you look like her."

"Do you think that bothers my dad?"

"What do you mean?"

"Like it makes him sad when he looks at me?"

Maria marveled again at the insightful question. Did Amanda remind Grady of his dead wife—the wife who had betrayed him? Did that affect the way he related to Amanda? Maria couldn't answer those questions. Despite all her reasons for not wanting to get involved in Amanda's life, Maria was drawn to the girl.

"Your dad loves you, so looking at you can only make him happy."

"Then, why does he yell at me all the time?"

Maria felt out of her element. "That's a question only your dad can answer. I would only be guessing."

"Then, what's your guess?"

Maria shrugged, wishing she had the nerve to tell Amanda that her attitude had a lot to do with how much her father yelled. "Probably because he loves you and doesn't want you to make bad decisions."

"But does he have to yell?"

"Maybe he thinks you aren't listening."

"I'm listening. I just don't like what he says."

"That's the problem right there."

Amanda sighed. "Well, maybe he's not listening to me. He does what he wants without asking us how we feel. Like moving here."

Maria puzzled over the girl's statement. "I thought your dad had discussed the move with you."

"How would you know?" The belligerent Amanda had returned.

"Your dad told me he had bribed you with learning to ski and ride horses."

"Yeah, but it wasn't a discussion. It was more like 'we're moving and you can learn to ski and ride horses there.' We didn't have a choice."

Maria took in Amanda's sullen expression. Would the girl consider her thoughts on the subject, or would she reject them outright? Only one way to find out. "Sometimes life doesn't give us choices. We just have to go with the flow."

Amanda shrugged. "What do you know about it?"

"Well, I had to move here for my job. All my family still lives in California. It was hard to leave them, especially since I had just spent the previous year away from them while I was on a mission project in El Salvador."

"You lived in El Salvador?"

"Yes."

"What was it like?"

Amanda's interest surprised Maria. "It's a beautiful country. I loved the people. If you'd like, I can show you pictures and some of the things I brought back with me."

"Maybe." Shrugging, Amanda quickly tempered her excitement as if she realized her question wasn't in keeping with the image she wanted to project.

"Just let me know."

"Sure."

They fell silent, Amanda seemed to focus her attention again on the double doors straight ahead. Noise from the TV continued to fill the otherwise quiet room. Maria tried to make sense of Amanda's behavior. She hopscotched from belligerence toward her father to genuine concern for her sister. Maria couldn't figure the girl out. Maybe the teenager didn't know her own mind, either.

While she stewed over Amanda's conduct, Grady strode through the double doors.

Amanda jumped up and greeted him. "How's Kelsey?"

Surprised again by Amanda's actions, Maria remained seated, watching the interaction between father and daughter. She couldn't miss the genuine affection he displayed toward his older daughter as he put an arm around her shoulders and spoke so quietly that Maria couldn't make out the conversation.

After Grady finished speaking to Amanda, he looked up, searching the room until his gaze fell on Maria. "Everything's going to be all right."

Maria stood and approached the twosome. "Did she break her arm?"

He nodded. "Just above the wrist. They're putting the cast on now."

"Can I see her?" Amanda looked up at her dad.

Grady gave Amanda's shoulders a squeeze. "After the doctor's done."

"How's she doing?" Maria asked.

"Okay. She's in some pain, but they've given her a painkiller that should work soon. She's taking it all in stride. She's already planning to collect signatures on the cast."

Amanda frowned. "That's dumb. Who does she know here?"

"She knows you, me, the doctor and nurses, Clay, Beth, Max, Sam, Jillian and Maria," Grady replied, gesturing toward her.

"Yeah, me and Max and a bunch of grown-ups." Amanda's pout had returned.

"Well, if that makes Kelsey happy, why should you care?"

"Yeah, whatever." Amanda pressed her lips together.

Taking in the exchange, Maria read annoyance in Grady's eyes, though he was trying to smile at Amanda. And she didn't miss his uneasy expression when he glanced at her over the top of the girl's head. "I'm going back to check on Kelsey. It shouldn't be much longer before we can go."

Trying to give him an understanding smile, Maria nodded. "Take all the time you need. Amanda and I are just hanging out here."

As Grady disappeared behind the double doors, Maria tried once again to make sense of Amanda's mood swings. Maybe the girl just didn't know how to handle change in her life.

Something continued to tug at Maria, making it difficult for her to resist getting involved in their lives. She reminded herself that Amanda probably wasn't interested in her help, or in her opinion. So it would be better to keep her distance. Grady most likely wouldn't appreciate her interference, either.

Amanda resumed her seat and hung her head while Maria stood and watched. Did she dare say something to the girl? As Maria returned to the chair she had occupied earlier, a nurse, scurrying through the double doors, momentarily captured her attention. When she glanced back at Amanda, the girl was slouched in her chair, but worry etched lines across her pretty face.

She sat there in stony silence, but she finally looked up. "Why does he always take Kelsey's side?"

Maria studied her. Was that a rhetorical question, or did the teenager really want an answer? "Does he?"

"Yes, always." Amanda's voice rose to a full-fledged whine. "Kelsey's the baby, so she gets her way. No one ever considers what I want."

"Are you sure?"

Amanda straightened in her chair and looked at Maria. "Yes. She always gets what she wants."

Maria wished she had never acknowledged the question. Now she was right in the middle of something she didn't know how to deal with. "Why don't you talk to your dad about it?"

"I told you he never listens. He just says I'm imagining things."

Maria shook her head. "I'm sorry I can't give you an opinion. I haven't been around you enough to know."

"Well, just wait. You'll see for yourself."

Maria was rescued from having to make a comment when Grady and Kelsey walked into the waiting area. With her arm in a sling, Kelsey sported a hot-pink cast.

Using her good hand, Kelsey thrust a pen at Maria. "You wanna sign my cast?"

"Sure." Maria took the pen. "Where?"

"Any place you want."

Looking over the cast, Maria read the signatures already scrawled across the uneven surface of the fiberglass. "I'll take this spot right here by your thumb."

"That's a good spot," Kelsey said as she held out her arm. When Maria finished signing, Kelsey turned to her sister, who was still sitting in the chair. "You can sign, too."

Without saying a word, Amanda went over to her and took the pen. She drew a big smiley face on the middle of the cast and signed a big *A* underneath it.

"Hey, that's cool." Kelsey smiled at her sister.

Maria released the breath she'd been holding, as Amanda looked her way. The expression on the teen's face seemed to beg for approval. Were her actions those of a child who was pleading for praise? Maria cautioned herself again against getting drawn into their problems.

"Okay, let's go home," Grady said, ushering Kelsey toward the door.

Maria followed. Moonbeams filtering through a thin layer of clouds added a glow to the security lights that illuminated the parking lot. Amanda scurried by and joined Kelsey as she walked ahead.

Grady fell into step beside Maria. She reached into her pocket and pulled out his car keys. "Here."

He waved the keys away. "You drive. That way I'll be able to keep an eye on Kelsey."

"Okay," she said. "It looks like Kelsey's doing pretty well. You must be relieved."

Nodding, Grady glanced her way. "It looks that way. I hope she can sleep tonight without any problems.

"She's probably so tired she'll sleep like a baby."

"I hope you're right." He paused. "I sure appreciate your help."

"I didn't do anything except sit and wait."

"Well, that was important, especially for Amanda. She needed you there so she didn't have to wait alone. Besides, she needs a woman's influence in her life." Grady hesitated again. "I have to confess, most of the time I don't know how to relate to a teenaged girl, even though she's my daughter."

Maria chuckled. "Do any of us understand teenaged girls?"

"Well, maybe not." Grady laughed, too. "I was hoping Beth might be able to befriend Amanda. So far, Amanda hasn't complained about spending time with Clay and Beth. Do you think Beth would do it? Should I ask her?" Grady didn't wait for Maria to answer. "After all, she has a teenaged son."

"I'm sure Beth and Clay will help however they can." It bothered Maria that Grady hadn't considered her as someone who could be friends with Amanda. But she should be glad, she told herself. She didn't need to get caught up in this family's problems. Besides, Beth was family. And as far as Grady was concerned, Maria was a business associate, nothing more.

"Yeah, but I'm hesitant to ask, because I don't know Beth very well."

"Have Clay talk to her," Maria said when they reached the car. She punched the keyless remote. The horn honked and the car lights flickered.

Grady looked at her over the top of the car as he opened the door for Kelsey. "That's a thought."

"It can't hurt," Maria said as she slipped behind the steering wheel.

Grady settled into the front passenger seat and buckled his seat belt. "Amanda, help Kelsey with her seat belt."

Amanda mumbled something unintelligible. Then the click of the seat belt sounded from the backseat. Wondering again what was going through Amanda's mind, Maria started the car. Just moments ago the girls had been peacefully talking to each other. Now Amanda seemed irritated. Maybe she didn't appreciate Grady's command to help her sister. Whatever the reason, Maria reminded herself, she wasn't going to find a solution to the girl's problems, because they weren't her business.

"You doing okay, Kels?" Grady asked as Maria turned the car onto the street.

"Yeah, Dad, but I'm tired."

"We're all tired. It's been a hectic day. Do you think you'll be able to sleep?"

"I guess, but my hand throbs."

Grady turned to look into the backseat. "We'll put some ice on it when we get home. The pain medicine should start working soon."

Kelsey didn't reply, and the only noise in the car

came from the hum of the motor as Maria made the short drive from the hospital to the house. After she pulled the car into the garage, Grady helped Kelsey out of the backseat and carried her to the porch.

He turned to Maria as she approached. "Could you unlock the door?"

Putting the key in the lock, she tried not to let the image of Grady holding his daughter lure her further into this man's world. She began to feel as though she was fighting a losing battle. How could she not be drawn into their family circle, when she lived right upstairs?

Maria unlocked the door and let it swing open. Without stopping, Grady carried Kelsey back to the bedroom. Amanda shuffled into the kitchen and closed the door behind her. Maria stood just inside the door and wondered whether she should stay or leave. Would she appear rude if she slipped upstairs to her apartment without saying goodbye? While Maria puzzled over what to do, Amanda opened the refrigerator and pulled out a can of soda, then plopped onto a chair.

Pulling the tab on the can, she glanced up at Maria. "You want one?"

Maria wanted to refuse, but maybe this was Amanda's way of making it known that she was willing to talk or that she wanted company. "Sure."

Amanda gestured toward the refrigerator. "Help yourself."

Maria grabbed a soda, wondering whether she had misread Amanda's invitation. What was there about the sullen teen that had her wanting to stick around? Did she see a little of herself in the girl—a girl who tried to gain her father's attention without success?

Trying to think of a topic of conversation, Maria sat

on the chair nearest to Amanda and opened the can of soda. The pop of the tab and subsequent fizz filled the otherwise quiet room. The two of them sipped their drinks in silence while Maria continued to search for something she could talk about with Amanda. She had already brought up the subject of school without getting an answer from the girl, but maybe with Kelsey out of the picture, Amanda might be more responsive.

"Kelsey told me about her school. What about you?"

"Do you really care?"

"Yes."

Amanda shrugged. "What can I say? It's school. I have to go whether I like it or not."

"True, but you might as well make the best of it. Do you have any special interests?"

"Like what?"

"Um…like music, sports, drama, art?"

Amanda wrinkled her nose. "You mean the nonclassroom stuff?"

"Yes." Maria didn't miss the awareness that flickered across the girl's features. Something in that list appealed to her. But would she reveal it?

Just when she was about to speak, Grady appeared in the doorway and the moment was lost. "Well, Kelsey's ready for bed," he said. "I need some ice to put on her hand. The doctor said we should ice it for about twenty to thirty minutes." He went to the refrigerator and pulled out the ice bin from the freezer, then turned to Amanda and pointed across the room. "Get me one of those big Baggies from the drawer over there."

With a scowl on her face, Amanda did as her father commanded. He seemed oblivious to her attitude as he took the bag and filled it with ice. Maybe he was just so concerned about Kelsey that he had no idea how he sounded when he barked out orders to her. Or maybe he was just used to telling people what to do and having them do it.

Maria stood. "Is there anything I can do?"

Grady glanced at her. "No, but thanks for all your help earlier tonight."

"Well, then, I guess I'll be going." Maria drained the last of her soda, then turned to go. "I'll see you at work."

"Sure."

As Maria started to leave, Kelsey appeared in the doorway between the kitchen and dining room. "Are you going to leave without saying good-night to me?"

"I thought you were almost asleep. I didn't want to disturb you."

Kelsey looked at her father. "Daddy, is it okay for Maria to stay while you read me a story?"

Nodding, Grady glanced her way. "You're welcome to stay if you want."

"If Kelsey wants me to stay, I will."

Kelsey took Maria's hand. "Yes, stay."

"Okay." Wondering how she had managed to get involved here, Maria let the little girl lead her toward her bedroom.

With apprehension closing in around him, Grady watched them go. He didn't need Maria's presence messing with his mind. Having her here would only remind him that his girls needed a mother. And he wasn't about to make *that* happen. But for Kelsey's sake, he would get through this evening.

"What am *I* supposed to do?"

Grady turned at the sound of Amanda's voice. Unhappiness dripped from every word. While he dealt with one child, he was failing another. Could he possibly persuade Amanda to deal kindly with her sister? Earlier tonight he had seen concern for Kelsey in Amanda's eyes, but now she just looked miserable. "What do you want to do?"

"Go back to California."

Grady released a harsh breath. "Well, that's not going to happen, so you'll have to make the best of it. Please be reasonable."

"What's *reasonable?*"

"I don't have time for this discussion." Grady turned to go.

"You never have time for me."

Grady stopped, his shoulders sagging. Parental responsibility weighed heavily on him. She was laying guilt on him, just to be difficult. Kelsey needed him more than Amanda right now. Why didn't she understand that? What would it take to appeal to her better nature? He gazed at his daughter, who looked so much like her mother. "Amanda, please understand that I have to take care of Kelsey. This move hasn't been easy for us and now things have gotten a little more difficult because of Kelsey's arm."

"Yeah, you're always taking care of Kelsey. I don't count. You don't care that I hate it here or that you took me away from all of my friends." Amanda crossed her arms and glared at him.

"You'll make new friends." Grady didn't add that he was glad to have taken her away from friends who, from all indications, weren't the kind she needed.

"No, I won't."

"Well, it'll make your life easier if you at least

give it some effort. We're certainly not going to solve this problem now. I'm going to take this ice in to Kelsey and read to her like I promised." He turned to go, then stopped and turned back to Amanda. "You can join us or—"

"I'll stay here," she said before Grady could finish.

"Suit yourself." Grady tried to block Amanda's belligerence from his thoughts. He was probably handling this all wrong, but he didn't know what else to do.

When he reached the bedroom, he stopped for a moment and watched Maria with Kelsey. There was no doubt that Kelsey had already adopted Maria as her friend, if not more. The two of them sat on one of the twin beds covered with pink-and-green floral comforters while they looked over Kelsey's stamp collection.

The overhead light shimmered in Maria's dark hair as it fell in soft waves around her shoulders. Why was he constantly noticing how beautiful she was? It seemed to happen quite frequently now that she had set the record straight about what had happened with Nina. But he was finding himself drawn to more than just her beauty. She had a kind and helpful spirit, which she demonstrated tonight by her willingness to remain here at Kelsey's request.

"Ready for this ice?" He held up the bag as he entered the room.

Looking up, Kelsey nodded. "Okay. Will it hurt?"

"No, we'll put a towel around the bag before we put it on your cast." Grady stepped into the adjoining bathroom and brought out a towel. "Okay, Kels, hop into bed, and you can sit with this ice on your arm while I read."

"Can I help?" Maria asked, getting up from the bed.

"Sure. Get that book lying on top of the bookcase."

Grady motioned toward the corner of the room with his head. He quickly wrapped the towel around the bag of ice and placed it on Kelsey's arm.

Maria held up the book. *"On the Banks of Plum Creek?"*

"That's it." Kelsey nodded.

Maria smiled as she handed Grady the book. He took it, and their gazes met and held. What was going through her mind? She was staring at him almost as if she couldn't believe he would take the time to read to his own child. She had good reason to think that. Until they had moved here, he had never spent time reading to his children. He wanted to make up for the years when he had worked rather than spending time with his family. He wanted to make a change in his life. This was a new beginning.

"Okay. Let's get started." Grady sat on the edge of the bed near the headboard, so that he was sitting beside Kelsey. He opened the book to the bookmarked page.

Maria sat opposite them on the other bed. "I read that book when I was a girl."

"You did?" Kelsey's eyes grew wide, as if she couldn't believe the book had been around that long.

"Yes, I loved them all. Have you read the other books in the series?"

Kelsey nodded. "Grandma Reynolds read them to me last year. Now Daddy does it."

Grady began to read, and Kelsey snuggled closer and laid her head against his arm. Tenderness for his child moved him and his voice cracked. He cleared his throat, trying not to let Maria know the emotions that nearly overwhelmed him. He wished Kelsey hadn't invited her to stay. She was intruding on his private time with his daughter. He shook the selfish thought away as he continued the story.

When he was halfway through the chapter, he glanced over at Kelsey. Her eyes were closed. "Kels?" he whispered. She didn't move.

"Is she sleeping?" Maria asked in an equally quiet voice as she leaned forward.

"I think so." He slipped the bookmark into the novel and laid it on the nightstand next to the stamp album. He stood carefully, so as not to disturb his sleeping child. She barely moved as he took away the ice bag and tucked the covers under her chin. He leaned over and kissed her cheek. "Sleep tight, sweetheart." Motioning for Maria to follow, he tiptoed out of the room. Once they were outside, he carefully closed the door. "Thanks for all your help."

"It was nothing. I was glad to do it." Maria made a move toward the kitchen. "Guess I'll be going."

"I'll see you out." Grady followed Maria. When they entered the kitchen, he glanced at Amanda, who slouched in a nearby chair as she listened to her iPod. He frowned at her. "Sitting like that isn't good for your back."

"Who cares?" Amanda slouched more.

"I do."

"Yeah, sure."

"Your sister's asleep, so be quiet when you go to bed. Okay?"

"Yeah, I wouldn't dare wake up the princess."

"Amanda, that's enough." Grady wanted to crawl into a hole somewhere. What must Maria think, when Amanda talked to him with such disrespect? He could run an organization, but he couldn't control his own child. What did that say about him?

Amanda bobbed her head up and down to the music he couldn't hear. "Okay, Dad."

Amanda's acquiescence was more of a dismissal than obedience to his request. If only he could escape to a place where his troubles would disappear. He didn't want to face Maria, but he needed to talk with her. Being with the kindhearted beauty was just as much a trap as remaining with Amanda and her belligerence. Amanda ensnared him in anger. Maria entangled him in her charm and made him want something from her that would only bring them trouble. The two females unnerved him. But he needed Maria's help. She had helped him tonight, mostly as a favor to Kelsey. Would she be willing to help *him* after the way he had treated her? There was only one way to find out.

Chapter Six

$\smileleaf$

Watching the exchange between Grady and Amanda, Maria maneuvered closer to the back door. The heated discussion was a continuation of their animosity from earlier in the evening. She certainly wasn't an expert on children and had no place telling a parent how to deal with a child, when she had no children of her own. But Grady wasn't helping himself by criticizing the way his daughter sat. Did he realize that? Probably not, or he wouldn't have said it.

Maria had wanted to say good-night to Amanda, but how could she interject herself into the conversation? Bowing out quietly appeared to be the best option. Putting a hand on the doorknob, she looked back at the dueling twosome. "Hey, good night, Grady and Amanda. I'm headed upstairs."

Amanda waved without ever missing a beat of her music. Grady moved swiftly to the door and held it open for her. "Could I talk with you for a minute?"

"Sure," Maria said, wondering what he could possibly have to say that he hadn't said to her earlier.

"Let's go outside." He nodded for her to precede him.

"Okay." Maria stepped onto the porch.

After he closed the door behind them, he stood there for a moment, not saying anything. A dog barked in the distance and a car passed along the quiet street, its headlights beaming into the darkness. She gazed at him, but he wasn't looking her way. He was staring back into the kitchen through the window in the top of the back door.

Without turning her way, he shook his head. "I apologize for Amanda's behavior. You shouldn't have had to listen to her tirade."

"I understand. She's not happy about moving here."

He spun on his heel and looked at her. "Did she tell you that?"

Maria shook her head. "She didn't have to. It's obvious from her behavior."

Grady sighed. "She's being completely unreasonable. No matter what I say, she's on the opposite side."

"Maybe if you tried to find something that interests her here, she would be more cooperative."

Grady laughed halfheartedly. "I'm afraid her only interests are boys and that iPod, and I'm not too excited about promoting either of those two items."

"Since she likes to listen to music, maybe finding an outlet for her musical interests would be good."

"Who knows what she's listening to on that thing?"

Did she dare tell him he ought to know what was on his daughter's iPod? "Maybe you should find out."

"You mean like snoop into her stuff?"

"No," Maria replied, shaking her head. "Just ask to look at it."

"And she'll probably tell me to leave her stuff alone."

"That's a good possibility."

"Then, there's not much I can do about it. Besides, I didn't want to talk to you about Amanda's problems." He waved his hand in the air, as if he were trying to erase the whole conversation. "I wanted to talk about Kelsey."

"What about her?"

"Well, the doc told me she has to keep her cast dry, and that means not getting it wet when she takes a bath." Grady hesitated, his mouth half open, as if the words wouldn't come out. "She's getting to be that age where she doesn't want her father helping her with her bath—if you know what I mean. But I need to make sure she doesn't get that cast wet." He paused again. "Could you… Would you…"

"Help her when she takes a bath?" Maria finished for him.

Relief spread across his face. "Yes, do you think she'd mind? She's a pretty responsible kid, but I'd feel better if someone was there to make sure it didn't get wet. I'd ask Beth, but they live so far from town now. I'd even have Amanda do it, but you've seen her attitude. So I don't even want to attempt to involve her. I hate to impose on you—"

"Grady, it's all right." Maria touched his arm for a second. "I do understand. And you're not imposing. I'd be glad to help Kelsey if she's willing. Have you asked her what she thinks?"

He shook his head. "You think I need to?"

"Yes." Maria nodded. "She probably doesn't want you to help her, but she might not be so eager to have me help, either."

"Hmm. I never considered that." His blue eyes searched her face. "If she's willing, would you mind?"

"No. I've always enjoyed being with your girls."

"Even Amanda?"

"Yes, even Amanda."

"I'm sure Amanda was much more pleasant when she was younger." He smiled wryly. "You used to babysit with them a lot when Nina was alive, didn't you?"

"Yes, I did."

Lowering his gaze, he rubbed the back of his neck. "I'm sorry I rebuffed you after Nina's death. It's come back to haunt me in so many ways."

"Didn't you tell me during our first meeting that rehashing the past isn't going to change anything? So why are you doing it now?"

Grady looked up, a little smile curving his lips. "You're right. I need to take my own advice and just move on."

"And I'll help however I can."

"Thanks. I'm just worried about Kelsey starting school with her right arm in a cast. She's right-handed. I guess she can still hold a pencil."

"I'm sure her teacher will understand."

Grady nodded. "Yeah, you're probably right. Kelsey already loves her teacher. That'll help. Wish I was as optimistic about Amanda."

"Speaking of Amanda, I just had an idea about how you can find out what's on Amanda's iPod."

"How?"

"Do *you* have an iPod?"

Grady knit his eyebrows and placed his index finger on his chest. "You mean me personally?"

"Yeah."

"No."

"Well, if you get your own and have her help you download some music, you might see what's on hers. Plus, you can give her the attention she wants so desperately."

"You think that would work?"

Maria shrugged. "It's worth a try."

"That means shopping. I don't have time to run into Spokane."

"Who says you have to go to Spokane? You can order one online."

"I haven't bothered to get Internet service here because this is only temporary." He gestured toward the house.

"You can use mine. Why don't you do it right now?"

Hesitating, he looked toward the kitchen, then back at Maria. "I suppose I could do that, but I need to tell Amanda first."

"Sure. I'll go ahead and log on and find a site where you can order one."

"Okay, I'll be up in a minute."

"Don't bother knocking. Just come on in," she called after him.

Maria climbed the stairs to her apartment. How had she managed to do the exact opposite of what she had planned? Taking care of Grady's kids was near the bottom of the list in her book. But she had seen a different side of the man tonight. She had seen a concerned father, an uncertain man and a lost soul. He wasn't the pompous know-it-all she remembered. Despite all her vows to make time for herself, she couldn't turn her back on people who needed her help, and especially not those motherless girls. She was getting herself deeper and deeper into their lives. *God, is this what You've intended for me? To help Grady and his girls?*

The prayer lingered in her mind while she waited for Grady. She went to the spare bedroom, where she had her computer set up. She brought up the Web site and scrolled through the information. Hearing the door open and close, she went into the hallway. "I'm back here."

He came around the corner into the hallway. When she saw him, her heart skipped a beat. This was not good. Turning back into the spare bedroom, she closed her eyes and tried to calm her racing pulse. She had no business reacting this way to the man. Helping Amanda and Kelsey should be her only concern. She couldn't let any tender feelings toward their father take root in her mind.

"So this is it?" he asked.

"Yeah." She couldn't help noticing how strong his hand looked as he pointed to the screen. When he sat on the chair in front of the computer, she shook the thought away and made a move toward the door. "I'll leave you alone so you can look this over and place an order if you want."

He looked over his shoulder at her. "Don't leave. I want your opinion."

"Okay." Her plan to escape disintegrated. She had no legitimate excuse to leave. In the small room, everything about him assailed her senses. His broad shoulders. His hand as it covered the mouse. His slightly disheveled hair. She tried to concentrate on the computer screen, but nothing erased his image from her mind. "What do you want to know?"

"Do you have one of these?" he asked, pointing to a picture of an iPod on the screen.

"Yeah, I use it when I work out."

"Where do you do that?"

"Didn't anyone tell you there's a fitness center at the office? Jillian believes it's important for her employees to stay healthy."

He shook his head. "Looks like you need to take me on a tour. I'm way too busy to work out, though."

The statement reminded Maria that this man was still a workaholic. She had to keep that in mind when her crazy feelings started interfering with her rational thoughts. He was bad news when it came to relationships. She planted that thought firmly in her mind.

"We'll do that on Monday." She caught herself before she almost invited him to join her when she worked out. That was the last thing she needed—to see Grady wearing athletic gear while pumping iron.

"Sounds good. Now, tell me which one of these you have."

"Sure." For the next few minutes, Maria helped Grady choose an iPod.

After he finished placing the order and printing out the receipt, he stood and stretched. "Thanks. I hope this will open a door with Amanda. If it doesn't, at least I'll have the latest gizmo. I'd better get back and check on the girls. See you Monday."

"You know, it wouldn't hurt to take the girls to church. It might be just what Amanda needs." Maria held her breath as she waited for his reaction. She didn't miss the irritation that flickered across his face before he smiled.

"Amanda's already made herself unwelcome with the church kids."

Maria frowned. "How?"

While they walked to her front door, Grady explained what had happened the night of the barbecue, when the girls went to the concert.

"That's too bad, but they'll give her another chance."

"But I won't." He narrowed his gaze. "People go to

church to worship. I'm not in the frame of mind to do that, and I don't see that changing. Besides, the church isn't a social club."

"But that's part of it. Sharing. Being friends. It's a family. And sometimes, just like in any family, there are squabbles."

"Well, I don't intend to be part of the squabbles. And I've seen that friendship thing ruin my marriage."

"I probably didn't state that very well." Maria sighed. "I'm sorry. I didn't mean to—"

"That's okay. You already know how I feel. I wouldn't change my mind, no matter how you stated it."

"The invitation is always there if you do."

"I won't." He opened the door. "Good night and thanks again."

"Sure. Good night." As she watched him descend the stairs, Maria tried not to let his opposition discourage her. His resistance to church would eventually hurt his girls. They needed to know the Savior, whether Grady wanted to or not. Would he let them go to church without him? Better not push. Maybe he would be more receptive some other time—like during the house-raising over the Labor Day weekend.

On Monday afternoon Maria glanced at her watch. Five o'clock. Where had the time gone? With a spring in her step, she left her office and walked down the hall to talk to Grady. Even though his office door was open, she knocked lightly on the door frame. Grady was sitting at his desk while he talked on the phone. Looking up, he motioned for her to come in, then concluded his conversation and hung up.

He smiled as he stood and shoved papers into the

open briefcase on his desk. "Good news. That was the general contractor for the center. All the inspections are complete, and he wants me to take the final walk-through. You headed home?"

"Yeah." Maria smiled, knowing they'd had a good day.

Not making eye contact, he continued to go through papers. "Amanda and Kelsey spent the day with Beth again, and she's dropping them off after she goes to the grocery store. I've called and told them I'd be a little late. I'm picking up pizza on my way home." Shutting the briefcase, he finally glanced up. "Would you mind checking in on them when you get home? Just to make sure they aren't trying to kill each other." He laughed halfheartedly.

"Sure. I'll check on them. They should be okay. They were getting along great last night, when Amanda volunteered to help Kelsey make sure she doesn't get her cast wet."

"That was a gift out of the blue. Most of the time I can't begin to guess what Amanda's going to do." Grady shook his head. "I never expected her cooperation."

"Maybe it was those prayers I said."

"No comment." He picked up the briefcase and headed for the door. "Oh, you're welcome to join us for pizza if you want."

Maria followed him into the hallway without responding to his invitation. Was he inviting her because he really wanted her to be there, or was he just being polite? And why was she worried about it, anyway? She should go just for Amanda and Kelsey's sake. "Thanks. I think I will. Pizza's one of my favorites, and I didn't plan anything for supper."

"Good. I've got to run. I'll see you later." Waving, he hurried out of the building.

As Maria drove home, she contemplated the evening ahead. Pizza with Grady and his girls. Why did it sound so appealing, when only a couple of weeks ago, just the prospect of meeting Grady face-to-face had her fearing the worst? Had her prayers brought on a change of heart about her goals? Maybe God was telling her it was more important to spend time with these lively girls rather than having time just for herself to curl up with a good book. How could she know for sure? God's leading wasn't always clear.

And what did spending time with Amanda and Kelsey mean for her unexpected attraction to their father? God surely wasn't at work there, was He? Grady was already displaying his workaholic tendencies, wasn't he? But she had to cut him some slack. This was a tremendously busy time, with the opening of the center just days away.

Maria started up the stairs to her apartment, but just then a car parked in front of the house. Maria stopped when she recognized Beth at the wheel. In a second, Kelsey popped out of the car, almost like a jack-in-the-box. In comparison, Amanda appeared to move in slow motion as she exited.

The passenger-side window lowered. "Hey, Maria," Beth called as she waved. "Grady said you'd be here when I dropped Amanda and Kelsey off. Good timing. I've got to rush. Clay's expecting me at home."

"See you later." Maria waved as Beth drove off. Kelsey joined her on the porch and grabbed hold of her arm. "Daddy says you're going to eat pizza with us. I'm glad."

Smiling, Maria nodded, thinking how nice it was to be wanted. "Me, too."

"Look at my cast." Kelsey held her arm out. "Max had the whole football team sign it. Even the coach. Cool, huh?"

Maria tempered a laugh. Was there anything that didn't excite Kelsey? "Yeah. Cool."

"That thing's going to be black instead of pink if she keeps collecting signatures." Amanda brushed past them and let herself into the house.

"You're just jealous because all the football team signed my cast." Sticking out her tongue, Kelsey pranced into the living room and twirled around. "So there."

Hurrying after the girls, Maria decided it was a good thing she was there. "Do you girls have chores or anything you have to do?"

"Nope." Plopping down on the couch, Amanda sat in her usual slouched position with her blue-jean-clad legs sprawled out in front of her. "Dad just said to behave ourselves until he got home." Amanda looked up at Maria. "Is that why he sent you over? To referee?"

"Do you need a referee?" Maria asked, hoping to catch the girl off guard.

Amanda straightened. "No."

"Then, I guess, he didn't invite me over to referee. Maybe he invited me because I like pizza."

"Well, don't be surprised if he calls and says he can't make it." Amanda slouched again.

Maria took in the girl's words, an ache in her chest. Would that happen? She had seen that pattern over and over again with her own father. Promises made but never kept. She didn't want to go through that again, and she hated to see Amanda and Kelsey go through it. Maybe

Amanda was wrong about tonight. Maria could only hope so. For now, she wanted to think of something more pleasant.

"Well, he said he'd be here right after he did the walk-through. That shouldn't take that long," Maria said.

"Yeah, sure. That's what he always says."

Maria didn't have a response to that. Maybe it was best just to ignore the girl's comments. "Hey, Kelsey, what did you do today?"

Kelsey immediately launched into a detailed account of their day with Beth, including their visit to football practice.

"Football's a dumb game," Amanda announced as she got up from the couch. "I'm going to my room."

"It's my room, too."

"Well, right now it's mine, so stay out."

"No." Kelsey dashed into the bedroom and closed the door before Amanda had crossed the room.

Maria stood there, dumbfounded. She was seeing a side of Kelsey she had never seen before. Possibly some of Amanda's complaints concerning her sister were warranted. Maybe Kelsey got away with things because she was the younger one. Grady might let things slide with Kelsey that he nailed Amanda for. How could she deal with it? These weren't her kids.

"Brat!" Amanda yelled, and pounded on the door.

This was trouble, and Maria had to step into the fray. She placed herself between Amanda and the door and gently took hold of her arm. "Amanda."

She frowned and stepped back. "What do you want? This isn't any of your business."

"Since I'm here, it is my business." Maria wished she

knew whether this was the right approach to take. How would Grady feel about this? But he wasn't here.

"So what are you going to do about *her?*" Amanda pointed at the closed door.

Her question refocused Maria's thoughts on the present. "The question is, what am I going to do with both of you."

"And what's that?" Defiance dripped from Amanda's every word.

"You'll find out. Go sit on the couch, please." Pointing toward the living room, Maria held her breath and waited for Amanda's response.

The girl mumbled something under her breath, but she went into the living room and plopped onto the couch.

Slowly releasing her breath, Maria tapped on the bedroom door with her knuckles. "Kelsey, please come out."

The door creaked open. Kelsey stared at Maria through the narrow opening. "Are you mad at me?"

"Only if you don't come out."

Kelsey let the door swing open to its full width and stood there, her head lowered. "I'm sorry. Don't tell my dad I was bad."

"I accept your apology, but I think you should tell him."

Kelsey's head popped up and her eyes grew wide. "Please don't make me tell."

"I'm not going to make you do anything except apologize to your sister."

"Yeah, brat."

Maria turned and impaled Amanda with a stare. "And *you* will *not* talk to your sister that way."

Amanda shrank back into the couch.

Maria gave Kelsey a little nudge toward the living room. "What do you say to Amanda?"

Her gaze downcast, Kelsey shuffled into the living room. "I'm sorry."

"Thank you." Maria glanced at Amanda. "Now it's your turn."

"Sorry." The word was barely audible, but at least she said it.

Looking at Kelsey, Maria tilted her head toward the couch. "Sit down next to Amanda."

Kelsey looked wary, but she did as she was told without saying another word.

Maria looked at the two girls, her gaze shifting from one to the other. What had happened to the camaraderie Amanda and Kelsey had shared just last night? Grady was right about not knowing what to expect. Maria wasn't sure Amanda and Kelsey should be left alone together if Grady had to work late. And she was pretty certain he had the same concerns. Thankfully, Beth seemed to have stepped in to help, but soon she wouldn't be available. What arrangements had Grady made for Kelsey once school started?

Maria pushed the question from her mind. These weren't her children. This wasn't her family. This wasn't her problem. She needed to quit taking on other people's worries. She had done that too much in her life. Grady could sort this out for himself. But she had to deal with it right now.

Amanda and Kelsey, appearing chastised, gazed back at Maria. What did she do now? *Lord, help me. Please give me wisdom in dealing with these girls.* The prayer gave her courage. "I didn't come here tonight to referee. I came to share the evening with you. Is this the way you behave around guests? Is this the way your father taught you to act?"

Neither of the girls spoke, but Amanda shook her head while Kelsey appeared ready to cry, pressing her lips together and blinking rapidly.

"Are you ready to treat each other and me with respect?"

They nodded in unison. Amanda sat forward. "You've been nice to us. I'm sorry I haven't been nice to you."

The apology made a lump form in Maria's throat. She had to swallow hard before she could speak. "Thank you, Amanda. I appreciate your saying that."

Quiet little sobs whispered through the room. Maria looked at Kelsey. Her shoulders were shaking and tears were trickling down her cheeks. The scene grabbed Maria's heart and wrung it out. She immediately sat next to Kelsey and gathered the child into her arms. "It's all right, Kelsey."

"No…it's…not," she said between sobs. She wiped her eyes with the back of her hand. "I'll have to tell Daddy."

Maria patted her on the back. "If you tell him, I'm sure he'll be proud that you told the truth and that you apologized. But it's your decision."

Kelsey gazed up at her. "Do you really think so?"

"Yes." Maria nodded. "Now, let's put all this behind us and have a good evening."

Before either of the girls could say anything, the phone rang. Amanda jumped off the couch and raced to grab the phone on the desk in the dining room. After she said hello, she listened for a moment and a sullen expression crept across her face. Finally, she looked at Maria and held out the phone. "It's my dad. He wants to talk to you. I told you something would come up."

Maria put the receiver to her ear, her stomach sinking with a sick sensation. "Hello."

"Maria." Even the way Grady said her name conveyed apology. "I'm sorry, but I'm not going to make it home until later tonight. I got tied up here with a huge problem. Something triggered the sprinkler system in one of the wings. Furniture, carpets, you name it—it's all soaked."

"Oh, no! Have you called Jillian? Do you need me to come over? Will everything—"

"Whoa! One question at a time. Yes, I've called Jillian. She and Sam are on their way right now." Grady paused. "And no, I don't need you to come over. I need you to stay with the girls, since you're already there. Can you do that?"

"Yes—"

"Great," Grady replied, not giving her a chance to put any qualifiers on her answer. "I told Amanda I ordered their favorite pizza. It should be delivered in about thirty minutes. It's all paid for. I'm not sure how long this is going to take, or when I'll get home. I sure appreciate your help."

"No problem. Will everything be ruined?"

"I hope not. I've got people here trying to clean up the mess and salvage as much as we can. Hopefully I'll see you soon."

"Hey, before you go—any instructions? Like bedtimes? Anything I should know about?" Maria listened as Grady gave her the information she needed. "Okay, I'll see you when you're finished."

"See? Now do you believe me?" Amanda asked as soon as Maria hung up the phone.

"This couldn't be helped. Your dad has a very good reason for being late. Did he explain?"

"Yeah. Said something about a flood. But why does something always have to happen? Why can't he have a good job that doesn't make him work late?"

Maria sighed. How many times had she asked that same question about her own father? Too many times to count. This whole evening was bringing back memories she didn't want to face. But Grady's girls needed her. She was determined not to let them down.

Chapter Seven

Grady pulled his car into the garage, turned off the engine and sat there in the dark. Leaning his forehead against the steering wheel, he took a deep breath. Here he was again, falling into the same pattern. He had promised himself things would be different with his new job. No long hours. No neglecting Amanda and Kelsey. Only a few weeks into the job, he had failed to live up to his own vow. Failed miserably.

Wasn't there a good reason? Yes, but hadn't he told himself the same thing a thousand times when he had to work late on a case at the law firm?

Now he had to face Maria. What must she think? That he hadn't changed at all? Her words echoed through his mind. *Did you ever think that might have been the problem? You were always working.* Didn't she already think he'd brought all his marriage difficulties on himself with his inattention? But tonight really was different. This had been a true crisis, one he couldn't ignore. He'd had a good reason for not coming home on time. She'd seemed to understand when they talked on the phone, but maybe she was only being polite.

A light high on a pole at one corner of the garage lit his path as he plodded toward the house. It was nearly midnight and the girls would be in bed, so he wouldn't have to deal with their disappointment, just Maria's. That was enough. But why was he so worried about her opinion, anyway?

Purging the question from his mind, Grady carefully opened the back door. The hum of the refrigerator and the ticking clock greeted him in the dark kitchen. The faint smell of pizza still lingered in the room. The quiet house only emphasized his distress over the situation.

He closed the door behind him and tiptoed into the kitchen. He didn't see Maria. He looked through the dining room into the living room beyond. The only light came from one small lamp sitting on an end table next to the couch. Maria sat in a chair, her back to him, her head bowed. Was she praying, or had her head lolled forward in sleep?

He stood in the doorway between the kitchen and the dining room. His apprehension made his feet feel glued to the floor. He didn't want to frighten her—or awaken the girls—by calling her name.

As if she sensed his presence, she suddenly raised her head and turned. "I thought I heard something." She stood and walked toward him. "So how did it go? Did they get everything cleaned up?"

No accusation filtered through her questions. A sense of relief bubbled up inside him as he nodded. "The company that deals with water damage did a good job cleaning up. We can be thankful this happened before anyone moved in."

"You're right."

"Are the girls asleep?"

Maria nodded. "They've been in bed since about ten."

"Even Amanda?"

"Yeah. We watched a movie. I let them pick from my collection."

"And what did you watch?"

"The Princess Diaries."

He had no clue what that movie was about. Maybe he should. All the events of the evening served to remind him that he hadn't really been part of their lives since they were born. Nina and a string of nannies had provided their care, while he stood on the sidelines. Oh, sure, his job was important, in that it provided the money they needed to live, but all those possessions couldn't make up for the time he hadn't spent with his kids. "Did they enjoy it?"

"Yeah, it's a perfect girls' movie. I hope you don't mind that I read another chapter from Kelsey's book." Maria chuckled. "Amanda even listened."

"That's a switch. And, no, I don't mind. Thanks. I just can't thank you enough. Having you here was a lifesaver."

"I'm glad I could help. Do you think we'll have to postpone the grand-opening celebration?"

Grady rubbed a hand over his stubble-covered chin. "No. We may have to replace some furnishings, but Jillian doesn't think we need to delay anything."

"We're good to go ahead with people moving in?"

Grady nodded. "Yeah, they'll move into the wing where there wasn't any damage."

"Do you know what caused the malfunction?"

"Not for sure. The company that installed the system is inspecting it." Grady didn't want to talk about the assisted-living center. He wanted to talk about why Maria was so understanding. But why borrow trouble? "Did you have any difficulty with the girls? I hope Amanda didn't misbehave like she did the other night."

Maria didn't say anything for a moment. She looked toward the bedroom door, then back at him. "We had a good time."

"That didn't answer my question," he replied, wondering what was behind her less-than-specific answer. "Did something happen that I should know about?"

"Like I said, we had a good time." Her gaze didn't meet his.

"Maria, you're sidestepping my question."

"I am?"

"You know you are. What happened here tonight?"

She closed her eyes. When she opened them, they welled with tears. "You—you have two precious children. I don't… Please, let's just forget about tonight. It's been hectic and crazy and, really, everything's fine."

For a moment he had the urge to pull her into his arms and comfort her, but that would be the last thing she would want. Pushing the thought away, he said, "You haven't convinced me."

"I know, but let the girls volunteer the information. And I mean, volunteer. Don't ask them. Please?" She sighed.

That little sigh touched something deep inside him. She cared about his kids. "Okay, I trust your judgment."

"Thank you." She placed her hand over her heart. "Believe me. It's for the best. And speaking of the best, have you talked to a Realtor about finding a place?"

Seeing a real estate agent. Another promise not kept. Another reminder of how he had let work occupy his mind, rather than his family. Why was she bringing that up now? "Is there some specific reason why you're asking that question?

"I just noticed how difficult it was the other night with the girls having to share a room. You had mentioned that it would be a source of conflict from the beginning." She shrugged. "And I just saw that you're right."

"I know. I know. I need to do that, but with everything that's going on at work I've just let it slide." Man. He hated admitting that to her. He stared at his feet. He didn't want to look at Maria for fear he would see disappointment in her eyes. "Next week should be a better week. The hiring's all done. I'll be moving my office into the center. We'll have staff orientation, and that should make for eight-hour days rather than ten or twelve."

"Well, I should be going."

"Yeah, it's late. Sorry to keep you up."

"I'm glad I was able to help out." She smiled and slipped outside.

Grady watched her disappear around the corner of the house. Her footsteps on the stairs sounded in the quiet. He knew she was safely in her apartment when the door opened and closed. He probably should have walked her to her apartment, but he had been afraid to spend more time with her. He was having a lot of romantic feelings about this woman. Maybe it all stemmed from her attention to his children. He should remember that. She cared about his kids, not him.

And had he apologized enough tonight? He was stumbling all over himself to get in her good graces and constantly seeking her approval. Every time he looked at her, these days, he saw more than a business associate. He saw a beautiful woman. That would be fine if the thoughts stopped there. He kept having these crazy feelings that might have caused him to do something like kiss her. Really crazy.

Grady peeked into the girls' room. The shaft of light beaming through the opening illuminated their sweet faces as they slept. They looked so innocent in their sleep.

And that was another problem. Whenever Maria was around Amanda and Kelsey, he couldn't help thinking how well they related to her. Her kindness toward them touched his spirit. She had cared for them even when he pushed her away. She had prayed for them. Was that what she'd been doing tonight when he'd returned?

Sam and Jillian had prayed tonight for God to help them with the crisis at the assisted-living center. Their prayers seemed to have been answered as everything in the cleanup process fell into place. Sometimes Grady wondered whether praying could help him with his girls, especially Amanda. Maria said prayer always did some good, but he couldn't bring himself to pray. How could he begin to trust a God who had allowed his wife to run off with another man?

The Friday evening before Labor Day, Maria stood on Sam and Jillian's deck. Conversation buzzed around her as a steady stream of people arrived to help frame the two new houses for the children's homes. She held her breath every time a car rumbled up Sam and Jillian's drive. Every time the car wasn't Grady's, a pinprick of disappointment flitted through her mind. She had to quit worrying about whether Grady and his girls would show up for the weekend.

There wasn't any reason they couldn't come. Kelsey's broken arm hadn't caused her any problems, so that shouldn't keep them away. Grady had indicated they would be here. Maria wondered whether he had found some excuse not to come. But why did she care, anyway?

Maria had to admit she had let her thoughts wander into unwise territory after Grady's invitation for pizza two weeks ago. She had been sucked into thinking he had changed after hearing him read to Kelsey. And even though he'd had a very good excuse for not getting home the night of the pizza invitation, the episode served to remind her that she shouldn't let any interest in Grady Reynolds settle in her heart. She knew his workaholic nature and, anyway, she wasn't interested in a ready-made family, despite her concern for his girls. Yet, here she was, wishing Grady would make an appearance.

"Hey, Maria," Jillian called as she wound her way through the gathering.

"Hey, yourself. Wow! You've got quite a crowd to work on the houses."

"I know. I keep wondering whether we'll have work for everyone," she said with a laugh. "Speaking of work, Grady told me that all the damage from the sprinklers was covered by the insurance."

"Yeah, I got his memo. And we're still set for the grand-opening celebration this coming Saturday. Grady said three couples are moving into the apartments in the unaffected wing next week."

"That's great." A little frown creased Jillian's brow. "Grady did say he'd be here, didn't he?"

Maria shrugged. "I'm not sure. Since he moved his office to the assisted-living center, I've only had work-related communication with him—e-mails and a couple of phone conversations. He didn't mention anything about this weekend."

"I know what you mean about not seeing people face-to-face. I've spent the whole week getting ready for this and I've done little else. I should've reminded him."

"I'm sure he remembers," Maria said, trying to convince herself of that. Why hadn't she reminded him? She was probably afraid her unintended interest might show. She couldn't help remembering how he had taken care of Kelsey and how much he wanted to understand Amanda. Hearing his voice over the phone reminded her of the look he had given her the night of the pizza invitation—a look that made her think maybe the interest wasn't all one-sided. Her pulse raced every time she thought of it.

"I'm just thankful we have wonderful weather. No rain in the forecast."

Jillian's statement made Maria look toward the sky.

"Me, too, since I'm sleeping in a tent."

"Did you bring your own?" Jillian asked.

"Yes, I learned as soon as I moved here that I should be prepared to camp at a moment's notice. So when my brothers asked me what I wanted for Christmas last year, I told them I wanted a camping tent. They couldn't believe it." Maria chuckled. "I'd better go set it up."

"Sure. See you later," Jillian replied with a wave.

While Maria got her tent and sleeping bag out of her car, she tried to brush away her disappointment that Grady might not show. Besides that, she missed Amanda and Kelsey—even their fights. Crazy.

She staked out a spot and began to set up the tent. As she secured the door flap, she heard her name and looked up. Kelsey came running down the hill, her hot-pink cast swinging in the sling.

Maria stood. "Hey, you'd better slow down, or you're going to fall on your face and break your other arm."

Kelsey giggled. "No, I won't."

"Well, you still better be careful."

"You sound like Daddy. He's always telling me to be careful, too." Kelsey gave her an exuberant hug. "I missed you. Did you stay away because we were bad?"

After Kelsey ended the embrace, Maria hunkered down in front of the little girl. "Oh, no, Kelsey. I would never do that. If you want to see me, just come up."

"I can do that?"

"Sure. Anytime."

"But, when I asked Daddy if I could visit you, he said you were probably busy."

"When you want to visit, just call me, okay?"

"Okay!" Kelsey clapped her hands, somewhat awkwardly because of the cast and sling.

Maria looked toward Grady's car. A fluttery sensation drifted through her midsection when she saw him talking to Clay and Beth. Amanda, dressed in skin-tight blue jeans and an equally tight knit top, leaned against the car, her head bobbing to the music on her iPod.

When Maria's gaze returned to Grady, he smiled and waved. That fluttery sensation took flight, as if a whole flock of birds had taken up residence in her stomach. She quickly returned her attention to Kelsey.

"How was your first week of school?"

"Good," Kelsey replied, nodding her head. "I like my new school way more than my old one."

"I'm glad." Maria glanced at Amanda. Did she share Kelsey's feeling, or did she still wish they hadn't moved here? Maria suspected the latter, because the teen's face was painted with that familiar sullen expression.

"Maria! Maria!" Kelsey tugged on Maria's arm.

"What?"

"I'm going to tell Daddy that we should put our tent beside yours."

"We'll ask him in a little bit. He may have other plans for your tent."

"No, he said I should pick out a place for it." Kelsey grabbed Maria's hand and pulled her toward Grady. "Let's go tell him."

"Okay." Maria's mind raced at the thought of having Grady nearby during the campout. Silly. He lived right upstairs, but there was something more intimate about being separated by sheets of nylon and mesh rather than wood and plaster.

Maria let Kelsey drag her over to Grady. He smiled again when he saw them approaching. Maria's stomach did that fluttery little dance for the umpteenth time. There must be something wrong with her mind when it made her think about this man in a romantic way. It must be her attachment to his girls that had her thinking in terms of romance. And that was even more senseless, given their tendency to fight.

"Hi," Maria said, feeling almost shy, while her insides went from fluttery to churning.

"Daddy, we can put our tent next to Maria's. See?" Kelsey said, pointing toward Maria's campsite.

Grady nodded. "Looks like a good spot to me. Let's get our gear."

"Maria can help, too." Kelsey skipped ahead to the car.

Grady gave her an apologetic grin. "I didn't mean that you should have to help us."

Maria fell into step beside him as he walked to his car. "I don't mind helping."

"Her enthusiasm sometimes scares me. It's almost like, if she doesn't let it out, she'll burst." Grady clicked his keyless remote, and the horn beeped.

"It's fun watching her enjoy life."

"You're right." Grady opened the trunk of his car. "Here's our stuff."

Maria took in the tent, sleeping bags, camp stove, lantern, chairs, a cooler with wheels and every other imaginable thing a camper would need. All of it new, still in the original packaging. "Looks like you're prepared."

"Yeah, that's why we're just getting here. The girls and I went into Spokane and did a little shopping." Grady lifted the tent out of the trunk and turned to Amanda. "Take this and have Maria show you where we're setting it up."

Amanda pushed herself away from the car and sauntered over to her father, her lack of enthusiasm showing in every step. "Sure."

"Daddy, what can I carry?" Kelsey held out her free arm.

"Here. Take the lantern."

Kelsey skipped ahead to Maria's tent. Grady used the wheeled cooler as a makeshift wagon and piled the rest of the gear on top. With her arms full of folded nylon camping chairs, Maria followed close behind.

With everyone helping, they made quick work of setting up the tent and the rest of the camping gear.

"Are we finished now?" Amanda asked, not disguising her irritation. "I want to hang out with my friends."

Grady nodded. "Yes, for now, but don't wander too far away."

"I wasn't planning to go on a hike—just talk to some friends," Amanda replied as she hurried away, sarcasm oozing from every word.

Grady didn't respond, but Maria read his annoyance in the set of his jaw. She also took in the information about Amanda's friends. Were they kids from church? Maria didn't think Amanda had connected with any of those kids, but maybe she had at school.

Grady turned to Kelsey. "Well, young lady, what are your plans?"

"I want to ride horses."

"How are you going to do that with a broken arm?" Grady asked, shaking his head.

"I do everything else." She put her free hand on her hip. "So I can do that, too."

"I don't know, Kels. They probably aren't doing that now. We're here to build houses."

"Your dad's right. Let me talk to Sam, and maybe I can set up a time when he can take you horseback riding." Maria glanced at Grady to get his reaction. "What do you think?"

"I don't know." Grady shrugged. "I don't want to impose. The horses are for the kids that live here, aren't they?"

"Yeah, but Sam conducts trail rides to earn money for the children's home. He has groups that come up all the time, especially through the summer and on weekends when the weather is good the rest of the year. And the kids at the home work to take care of the horses."

"Oh, so I can make arrangements to go horseback riding?"

Maria nodded. "I thought you knew that."

"No, but now I do."

"So that means I get to ride horses. Yippee!" Kelsey tugged on Grady's arm. "Dad, can I go see Sammy?"

"Okay, but be careful."

Kelsey skipped off without a backward glance, and Grady turned to Maria. "If only I had half her energy. That broken arm hasn't slowed her down at all."

Maria laughed. "Something to be thankful for, right?"

"I guess so. She just makes me nervous with all that jumping around."

Sometimes the things Grady said made Maria think that this man was just getting to know his daughters. And maybe he was. After all, hadn't he been an absentee father for all the years she'd been friends with Nina? And from what she had gathered from snippets of conversation, not much had changed after her death. At least now Grady appeared to be working on the relationship with his girls. But he had his work cut out for him with Amanda.

His effort to be a better parent touched her and made her think that maybe, just maybe, all those romantic thoughts she'd been having about Grady weren't so bad. Did she dare trust her feelings?

"I hope you don't mind our setting up camp next to you. Kelsey kind of has a way of pushing herself on people. And pushing her agenda. Like the horseback riding." Grady's comments brought an end to Maria's speculations.

"I'm sure I can help her with her agenda. And I don't mind having you camp next to me. It'll be just like home, having you for a neighbor."

"Well, I hope it's not exactly like home. Maybe the

presence of a crowd will keep Amanda and Kelsey from fighting." Grady grimaced. "I'm sorry about the way the girls acted the other night."

"Just the fact that they told you is a good sign." Peace settled in Maria's mind.

"Well, Kelsey confessed. Then Amanda owned up to her part in the fracas." Grady gave her a wry smile. "I wish they'd just get along."

"Raising kids is a hard job, especially today. There seem to be so many influences that parents can't control."

Grady looked past her, a faraway look in his eyes. "That's for sure."

Maria wanted so much to mention how the church's influence and prayer could make a parent's job easier, but she knew Grady's stance on the subject. If she brought it up too often, he might strengthen his resistance. *Lord, help me know when and how to talk to Grady.*

Wondering what he was thinking, she tried to follow his gaze. Then she noticed Amanda standing near the edge of the woods with another girl. Maria recognized her as one of the girls who lived at the children's home. The girl said something, and Amanda laughed. Had Amanda met this girl at school? Did she dare ask Grady? She decided against it. This wasn't any of her business. She had to quit letting herself get tied up in his family affairs. But something kept drawing her in against her will.

"You should've heard what Kelsey said to me the other night when she told me about fighting with Amanda." Grady's words seemed to come out of the blue.

"Are you going to tell me?"

He turned toward her, pain written on his face. "She said, 'Daddy, do you love me? Will you love me even when I'm bad?'" He paused and looked away. "How am I supposed to deal with that?"

"What did you say?"

He turned back, the pained expression still there. "I told her I'd always love her, no matter what, but just the fact that she asked the question killed me."

Maria didn't know what to say. Why was Grady telling her all this? Just weeks ago, he'd equated her with everything bad that had happened to him. Now he was using her as a sounding board about his kids. She didn't want to get involved. She was having enough difficulty keeping thoughts about him from turning into something more than she wanted them to. Maybe it was already too late. Even now, she was too attached to the girls to ignore their father.

"You know, kids say all kinds of stuff. They even tell you they hate you when things don't go their way. I'm sure Kelsey knows you love her."

"That's what I keep telling myself."

"Good. That's what you should do. Kids will be kids. They'll always find something to fight about from time to time."

"I know you said that before, but I guess I wasn't a typical kid."

"What do you mean?"

"I really don't remember fighting. Maybe because I was the oldest, I always did what was expected of me."

"Always?"

He quirked an eyebrow. "You doubt me?"

"Are you trying to tell me you never did anything your parents didn't want you to do?" Maria asked with a chuckle.

"Pretty much."

"I'm sorry, I'm having a hard time believing this. You're telling me that if I ask Clay he'll tell me you were the perfect child?"

Before Grady could answer, Sam's dinner bell rang across the yard and into the forest. "Sounds like the food's ready. And I'm ready to eat."

"You're ignoring my question. Does that mean Clay might give me different information than you're giving me?"

"No." A smug smile curved his mouth. "You can ask him while we eat."

"You're on," she said, and then realized she had just committed herself to eating with Grady. Not a wise move. Too much time with this man was going to undo all her resolve not to care for him.

Chapter Eight

The smell of grilling hamburgers and hot dogs filled the air as Maria and Grady joined the line that snaked around the yard. Kelsey followed, but Amanda hung back with her newfound friend. From time to time, Maria noticed, Grady cast a glance in their direction. Was he worried about Amanda's choice of friends, or was it just a father's natural curiosity? Maria itched to ask, but she focused her attention on something more mundane. "It's a big undertaking to feed all these people."

Kelsey glanced up. "Yeah, how many people do you think there are?"

"I couldn't guess," Maria said, smiling down at Kelsey.

"I'm going to count them," the little girl announced.

Grady chuckled. "That might not be so easy, when they keep moving around, but at least it'll pass the time."

While they worked their way toward the front of the food line, the conversation centered around the work ahead. Finally, Maria was able to focus her thoughts on something other than her growing affection for Grady Reynolds and his daughters. After they got their food,

Maria followed Grady and Kelsey to one of the many picnic tables scattered across the yard, where they joined Clay and Beth.

Grady settled on the bench, then glanced at Maria, who was sitting on the other side of Kelsey. "Hey, Clay, Maria has something she wants to ask you."

"What's that?" Clay looked over at Maria.

Maria shook her head. "Nothing, really."

"Hey, Daddy!" Kelsey said, pulling on Grady's arm. "I counted 211 people."

"Good going, Kels." Grady patted her on the back.

Thankful for Kelsey's interruption, Maria took a big bite of her hamburger and chewed slowly. When she finally looked his way, he winked and gave her a wry smile that told her he wasn't going to let the subject die. He was having fun with this. She didn't want that. She didn't want him to be jovial and relaxed. Jovial and relaxed threw her off guard and made her vulnerable to his unexpected charm.

"Daddy, why did you wink at Maria?"

"Because she's supposed to ask your uncle Clay a question."

Looking at Maria, Kelsey narrowed her gaze. "What are you supposed to ask?"

Grinning, Maria looked at Grady over the top of Kelsey's head. "Are you sure you want your daughter to hear this?"

"Absolutely."

Sighing, Maria looked at Clay. "Grady claims he never got into trouble as a kid and he says you can verify that."

Clay guffawed and then fixed his gaze on Maria. "Since he's six years older than me, I wasn't there for the first six years of his life and I don't remember the next six years of my life, or his, in any detail." Then he glanced at Grady. "But he's right. I can't remember him ever getting into trouble."

Grady grinned. "See. I told you so."

"Yeah, but we haven't accounted for a third of your life," Maria protested. "Is that really fair?"

"Do the first twelve years count?"

Kelsey tapped Grady on the arm. "I'm in my first twelve years and Amanda just finished her first twelve years."

Clay chuckled and gave Kelsey the thumbs-up sign. "She's got you there."

"Yeah, Dad."

Clay pulled a cell phone from his pocket. "Maybe we ought to give Trent a call. He's only a couple years younger than Grady. He probably remembers a lot and he can give us those details."

Grady shrugged. "Go ahead."

As soon as Clay punched in the number, Kelsey reached for the phone. "I wanna talk to Uncle Trent."

Clay handed her the phone. "Okay, kiddo. Ask your uncle what kind of kid your dad was."

Maria watched and listened as Kelsey gave Trent a blow-by-blow account of everything from her broken arm to the meal.

"Hey, Kels, get to the point," Clay said. "It's a good thing I have lots of minutes on that phone. Get the goods on your dad."

Kelsey finally asked the question about Grady, then listened intently. After a minute or so, she ended the call and handed Clay the phone.

"Well, what did he say?" Maria asked.

"He said to ask Daddy about Gramma's flower garden."

Grady knit his eyebrows. "Oh, that doesn't count."

Maria tried to hide a smile. "Why not?"

"Because I thought I was helping."

"So how did you help?" Clay teased.

"This really isn't fair, you know." Grady gave Clay a sour look. "I was going to weed her flowers and pulled the flowers instead of the weeds." He turned to Maria. "Does that make you happy?"

Maria pressed her lips together, still trying not to smile. Then she burst out laughing. She looked at Grady, who didn't seem amused. "I'm so sorry. I just couldn't help myself. That's so funny."

He flashed her a fake smile. "I'm so glad I could amuse you."

"That was pretty good." Clay joined in the laughter.

"Hey, you guys, quit picking on Grady." Beth poked Clay in the arm. "You're just jealous because you got in trouble all the time."

Clay put an arm around Beth's shoulders, pulled her close and gave her a peck on the cheek. "Not all the time."

"Daddy, why did Uncle Trent say you were an old man at ten?"

"He said that?"

"Yeah, what did he mean?"

Clay raised his hand. "I can answer that."

"I'm sure you can." Grady glared at his younger brother. "You guys are having too much fun at my expense."

"No, no. We're just trying to get you to lighten up. That's all." Clay ducked when Beth tossed a wadded-up napkin at him. "Okay, my wife thinks I've picked on you enough. But I do have to answer Kelsey's question."

Clay grinned at Kelsey. "Your uncle Trent means your dad was too serious when he was a kid. He didn't know how to have fun. He still doesn't. He works too hard."

"Then what am I doing here?" Grady asked.

"You're here to build houses. Sounds like work to me," Clay replied.

Grady held his hands up in front of him. "Okay, I give up. I'm just a big stick in the mud."

"No, you're not, Daddy," Kelsey said. "I think you're lots of fun, especially since we moved here."

Grady smiled and gave her a hug. "Thanks, Kels. Let's you and me go for a little walk."

Kelsey jumped up. "Okay."

As Grady and Kelsey walked off together, Maria watched them go with a better understanding of the man who had once intimidated her. As the oldest child, he had always been trying to please his parents. That probably made it doubly hard for him to understand his oldest daughter. Everything she was learning about him made her care that much more. Would she be sorry?

"How is it working with Grady?" Clay's question startled Maria from her thoughts.

"Oh, fine."

"No, I mean…is he still a perfectionist?"

Maria didn't know how to respond. So far she had found Grady to be organized, punctual, responsible. All good qualities. Did they spell *perfectionist?* "I'm not sure what you mean?"

"Sorry. That probably wasn't a fair question to ask." Clay grimaced. "Sometimes I worry about him. He's always been way too serious. He and my dad. Two peas in a pod. In fact, I think Grady was worse than my dad. Nothing was ever good enough for

Grady. It wasn't fun trying to follow in his footsteps. It was hard to live up to that example. I can still hear people saying, 'Why can't you be more like your brother Grady?'"

"People shouldn't compare siblings with each other." Beth gazed at Clay with an adoration Maria envied.

"You can say that again," Clay replied. "It's hard being a perfectionist. I think that's what drives Grady— that feeling that he's responsible for everything. It's almost as if he blames himself for Nina's death. He's never been the same since she died."

"I can see that." Maria was surprised to hear Clay's statement. She had no idea that Grady blamed himself. She had always thought he blamed everyone else. Clay had a completely different perspective, even though he didn't know all the circumstances of Nina's death. Could Clay be right? Did Grady blame himself?

"I'm hoping his move here will help change everything for him. He needs our prayers. And so do the girls." Clay glanced at Beth. "Beth's been trying to spend time with the girls and help them, but now that school's started, she doesn't have as much opportunity."

"Well, I've been praying, too." Maria smiled at Beth. "Maybe you and I could do something together to help the girls."

Beth nodded. "Yes, I'd like that."

"You know, Kelsey mentioned something about baking for the school's fall festival. We could do that. What do you think?"

"That sounds great."

Maria looked around for a moment, until she spotted Amanda sitting with her new friend. "I hope Amanda will be as excited about the opportunity as Kelsey."

"Well, from my observation, it's hard to get Amanda excited about anything," Clay said with a grimace.

"Has Grady ever said anything to you about either of the girls?" Maria asked.

"Grady doesn't say much about anything. I'm afraid he's bottled everything up inside, and that can't be good."

Beth placed a hand on Clay's arm. "But you can't force someone to talk."

Clay laughed and glanced at Maria. "She's saying that because she knows what it's like to do that very thing. Not wanting to talk."

"Yeah," Beth replied. "So I understand Grady's reluctance. He'll open up when the time is right. We just need to make it a matter of prayer, because sometimes God uses people in ways they never expect."

"We can both relate to that. I never imagined that Jillian's call for help with her foundation would lead me to Beth." Clay squeezed her shoulders. "Falling in love with this woman and a small town weren't part of my plans."

The sound of Sam's big cowbell clanged through the air and brought their conversation to a halt. When the crowd quieted, Sam stepped up to a microphone set up on the deck. He welcomed everyone and instructed several people to pass out schedules for the weekend. After everyone received an agenda, Sam called one of the men from a visiting church up to the deck and introduced him as the evening's emcee for karaoke.

Maria leaned across the table and whispered, "You mean, people actually want to get up and sing in front of a crowd?"

Beth giggled. "Well, not Clay. He'd clear out the entire grounds."

Clay shot Beth a perturbed look, but then laughed. "She's right. I can't sing, but there are lots of folks who can. So it's fun for them to sing and for the rest of us to listen."

"Well, you won't see me getting up there," Maria said, glancing around the grounds for Grady and Kelsey. She didn't see them because the fading sunlight made it difficult to see in the shadows.

She asked herself why she was even concerned about Grady, but she knew the answer. Something Clay had said made her wonder whether God had some purpose for bringing her and Grady together. Clay said Grady never talked with anyone about the girls or Nina, but he had done both with her. She had forced the issue with Nina, but he had volunteered the information about Amanda and Kelsey. Was he reaching out for help? And had God called her to be that help? The thought scared her. Helping could drag her into something she wasn't prepared to deal with—her attraction to Grady.

Suddenly Maria noticed Amanda walking across the yard toward the deck. When she stopped and talked with the emcee, Maria couldn't believe what she was seeing. Maria turned to Clay and Beth. "Is she going to sing?"

"Got me," Clay replied. "This is a surprise. She usually seems so detached and shy."

"Listen." Beth poked Clay in the ribs. He gave her a sheepish grin as the emcee gave Amanda a hand up to the deck.

"All right, folks, we're ready for our final singer this evening. Let's hear it for Amanda Reynolds, singing 'You've Got a Friend,'" the emcee said amid scattered clapping.

While the intro played, Maria leaned forward and

wondered what had prompted the sullen teenager to join in the karaoke. Despite the microphone, the first few words of the song were lost in the buzz of conversation from people who'd grown tired of the evening's lackluster performances. But as Amanda's clear, strong voice brought life to the song about friendship, the level of noise in the yard dropped until everyone was listening to the young beauty singing her heart out. She appeared to be lost in the music, just as she was so often while she listened to her iPod.

Her voice wound its way through the quiet forest as the audience sat mesmerized. Maria scanned the area for Grady, but she still couldn't see him. Did he know about Amanda's talent? What was he thinking at this moment?

When the last notes faded, applause erupted and echoed through the yard and the forest beyond. Amanda took a bow. Grinning widely, she looked at Maria. Then Maria followed her gaze as it settled on Grady. She didn't miss the pride on his face as he applauded with the crowd.

As Amanda made her way off the stage and back to the table where her friend sat, Grady made his way over to his daughter and gave her a hug. Kelsey hugged her, too. Seeing the sisters share a happy moment made Maria feel all warm inside.

"Wow! The kid can sing," Clay said. "She must've gotten her talent from her mom's side of the family."

"You mean Grady can't sing, either?" Beth asked with a chuckle.

"No, the Reynolds brothers have no singing talent. You don't want to hear us singing." Chuckling, Clay stood. "Let's go congratulate her."

Maria joined Clay and Beth as they made their way

over to where Amanda sat, still beaming from her performance. Grady's grin grew bigger as more and more people came over to express their appreciation for Amanda's singing. When several of the kids from the church youth group, including Max, stepped over to talk to her, Maria hoped this would be a new opening for her with these kids she had alienated with her attitude.

"That was terrific. Where'd you learn to sing like that?" Max asked.

Amanda shrugged. "I just sing."

A girl with red hair approached Amanda. "Hey, Amanda, I don't know if you remember me, but I'm Brittany."

Amanda nodded. "Yeah, I remember."

"Every year between Thanksgiving and Christmas, the church kids and some adults put on a program. With your beautiful singing voice, you really ought to consider helping us out. If you're interested, I can get you more information." With hope written on her face, Brittany gazed at Amanda.

"Okay," Amanda said, shrugging again.

Sam made his way through the crowd gathered around Amanda. "That was a great performance. We could use you to sing in the program the youth put on at church every year. I really hope you'll consider it?"

"Thanks. Brittany already asked me." Amanda smiled shyly. "I'll have to see what my dad says."

Surprised that Amanda wanted her dad's approval, Maria tried to gauge what Grady might be thinking about this invitation. Would he consent to Amanda being part of the church youth group? This was an excellent opportunity for her to use her talent. Surely, he would see the benefit. This was something Amanda needed. A place to fit in and friends, just like in the song.

Maria resisted the urge to become part of the chorus trying to persuade Amanda to join. She wanted to help the teenager make wise decisions, but pressure from too many sides might push Amanda the other way. Instead, Maria prayed that God would provide an opportunity for her to share with Amanda on a personal level. One-on-one.

Adolescence was such a difficult period in a person's life. How much more difficult it must be for a motherless girl. Heaviness filled Maria's chest as she remembered how much Nina, despite her infidelity, had cared for her girls. Maria had grieved over her friend's death. What must it have been like for these little girls, especially Amanda? She must have endured more grief than Kelsey. Amanda probably had more vivid memories of her mother than Kelsey because she was so much younger. And Kelsey seemed to have the kind of personality that let her survive the bumps in the road more easily than her sister.

While Maria let her emotions run the gamut, Sam called for everyone to gather in close to the deck, where he stood in the light shining from one corner of the house. He took the microphone, looked out over the crowd and expressed his thanks for everyone who had come to work. Then he led the group in a couple of choruses. Praises to God filled the night air, accompanied by crickets chirping in the night.

After the singing, Sam took his Bible and opened it. "I'm going to read from Luke 6:47-49. Jesus is talking here and says, 'I will show you what he is like who comes to me and hears my words and puts them into practice. He is like a man building a house, who dug down deep and laid the foundation on rock. When a flood came, the torrent struck that house but could not shake it, because it was well built. But the one who hears my words and does not put them into practice is like a man who built a house on the ground without a foundation. The moment the torrent struck that house, it collapsed and its destruction was complete.'

"We're here this weekend to build a couple of houses. If you go down the road, you'll find the foundations have already been poured. We've made sure we have a good foundation for them. I hope everyone here tonight will think about the foundation you have set for your life. Jesus wants you to make Him and His teachings the foundation for the things you do. Let the teachings of Jesus fill your mind while you're working this weekend. And after you leave here, let Him guide your life. Now, let's take a few minutes to ask the Lord's blessing on our work."

While Sam prayed, Maria couldn't concentrate on the prayer, because she wondered whether Grady was thinking about what Sam had said. She hoped the message would touch Grady's soul. Could he ever overcome his grief and come back to his faith? With so many prayers being lifted on Grady's behalf, how could he resist the calling of God's spirit?

When the prayers had ended, the group dispersed. Flashlight beams pierced the darkness as people traversed the grounds. Most people quietly made their way in the dark to their tents or campers as they planned to turn in early in preparation for the seven o'clock start time the next day.

As Maria prepared to enter her tent, Grady approached, with Amanda and Kelsey walking beside him.

Their flashlights bobbed as they walked. He glanced up when they drew near. "Hi. Getting ready to call it a night?"

"Yeah." Maria smiled and looked at Amanda. "I certainly enjoyed your song tonight."

"Thanks," Amanda replied, her head lowered and the toe of her sneaker-clad foot digging into the ground.

"Would you like to eat breakfast with us in the morning?" Kelsey asked. "Dad's fixing pancakes."

"Sounds good." Maria grinned at Grady. "Seems to me I've heard good things about those pancakes. I'll be there."

Kelsey tugged on Maria's arm to gain her attention. "If Daddy snores too loud, can I come sleep in your tent?"

Even in the dim light, Maria didn't miss Grady's embarrassed expression. "No, you may not sleep in Maria's tent. Behave yourself. Besides, I don't snore that loud."

"Oh, but you do, Dad." Amanda grinned up at him. "I hear you snoring through the walls."

Kelsey giggled and gave Amanda a high five. "Sometimes he sounds like a growling bear."

Grady frowned. "You're exaggerating. Your mother never complained."

"That's because she loved you."

For a moment Grady didn't say anything. He glanced at Maria. She didn't miss the pain in his eyes in the moment before he looked back at his girls. "And you don't?"

"Yes, I love you, Daddy." Kelsey flung her arms around her father.

"Hey, watch that cast. It's a weapon."

"Sorry." Still hugging him, she giggled some more.

He reached over and pulled Amanda into the embrace. "I love you, girls. And if I snore, just poke me. Okay, now you get ready for bed. Go." He gave them a little push in the direction of the tent.

When they were inside, he looked over at Maria. Although his face was in shadow, pain was still evident in his eyes. "They keep me on my toes."

"I can see that," Maria said, sensing discomfort in his tone and wondering whether he was still grieving over his loss. Was he still thinking about what Kelsey had said about Nina? Maria couldn't begin to relate to his pain. Maybe he just felt awkward because she knew about Nina's betrayal. The secret they shared would always bind them in an uneasy sense.

Maria had the sudden longing to comfort him. The urge was so strong that she knew she had to get away before she did or said something that would only make things worse—like throwing her arms around him and holding him close to ease his pain. The way he was looking at her made it difficult, but she forced herself to turn toward her tent. "I'll see you in the morning for those pancakes."

"Sure. Good night," he replied as she slipped into her tent.

After Maria got ready for bed, she lay in her sleeping bag. The night sounds of chirping crickets and quiet conversation reverberated around her. She heard Amanda and Kelsey giggling together. Their laughter warmed her heart. They weren't fighting. That was a good sign for Grady and for his daughters. This weekend together was doing a lot of good for everyone except her. So far, everything that had happened only served to confuse her and make her question her goals.

A deep-seated longing had inundated Maria when she watched the jovial yet poignant exchange between Grady and his daughters. An unexpected yearning had settled in her soul. A yearning for a family of her own.

She had thought she wanted something completely different. Time to be alone. Time for herself. Time without someone else depending on her.

Now she wondered. Somehow, tonight, lying in her tent alone didn't seem all that wonderful. This ache for something she didn't have was making her confused about her goals. What did she really want? Definitely not a man like Grady Reynolds, who put more time into his work than his family.

Yet Maria had seen a different side of Grady tonight. Maybe that was what had her completely disconcerted. But this change in his behavior might be only temporary. She had seen it too many times with her father. She had to keep the right perspective where this family was concerned. Despite her tender feelings for Amanda and Kelsey *and* their father, she couldn't let herself get too involved.

But Beth's words from earlier kept playing through her mind. "Sometimes God uses people in ways they never expect." Was God trying to send her a message? Did He have a different purpose for her, a purpose she wasn't expecting? For once in her life, she was afraid to pray for an answer, because that answer might not coincide with her plans.

Chapter Nine

On Sunday morning Grady stood outside his tent while Amanda and Kelsey dressed. The smell of frying bacon wafted through the cool morning air. Near Sam and Jillian's house, folks had already gathered for the breakfast being provided for all the workers. He wouldn't be making pancakes this morning.

Yesterday Amanda and Kelsey had helped him make pancakes and serve them to Maria. They had laughed and talked together in a way they hadn't done since the girls were much younger—since before Amanda had become a teenager. This weekend had made him realize he really didn't know his girls as he should. He was trying to be a better father. Make a new start. Could he continue in this path, or would he fall back into his old ways?

Then there was Maria. How was he supposed to deal with her?

Grady saw the way Amanda and Kelsey related to Maria and she to them. Surely, there was no harm in letting the relationship blossom. They needed a woman's influence.

"Good morning."

Grady spun around when he heard Maria's voice. She couldn't possibly know he'd been thinking about her, but warmth still crept up his neck when their gazes met. "Yeah, it is a good morning. Did you sleep well?"

"I did, but I've discovered muscles I didn't know I had, and they're a little sore this morning." She rolled her shoulders. "How about you?"

"Yeah, it's unbelievable how a little physical labor can remind you that you sit behind a desk all day."

Maria glanced toward Grady's tent. "Are the girls up?"

"They're awake, but they're moving slowly this morning. Even the young ones are feeling the effects of a hard day's work."

"Thankfully, we get to rest today. Then it's back to work on Monday." Maria chuckled. "We get to labor on Labor Day."

"It's really amazing what we accomplished yesterday. And the organization is incredible. Even the youngsters had jobs."

"Yeah. Jillian worked on several Habitat for Humanity houses and learned a lot from that. So she and Sam employed those techniques here." Maria flashed him a smile that seemed to turn him inside out. "Well, I'm off to the chow line. I'll see you at the worship service."

"I'd better get Amanda and Kelsey moving, or we'll miss breakfast." He stepped toward the tent without acknowledging Maria's reference to the worship service. How was he going to manage that? It would look bad if he didn't attend, but he hated being a hypocrite. While he stewed over that situation, he tried not to admit his own disappointment that Maria hadn't waited for them. He had enough to handle without worrying about her.

Amanda emerged from the tent. "Hey, Dad. We're ready."

"It's about time."

"I'm going to get Maria." Kelsey skipped ahead toward Maria's tent.

"She's gone," Grady called after her.

Kelsey stopped and turned. "How come she didn't wait?"

"Probably because she was hungry and you guys were taking forever to get ready."

Kelsey grabbed her dad's hand and dragged him toward the serving line. "Come on. Let's find her."

"Take it easy, Kels. She's probably got her food."

"Let's see." Kelsey continued to pull on his arm.

"Oh, all right."

Amanda fell into step beside him. "Dad, is it okay if I sit with my friend Courtney?"

"Is that the girl you've been hanging out with?"

"Yeah."

"That's fine." He watched Amanda hurry ahead and join her friend, who was already in line.

He should be glad Amanda had asked permission, instead of just storming off in her usual manner, but he wasn't. He was still worried about this girl and why Amanda had befriended one of the kids who lived at the home—admittedly, kids who had problems. Would this girl have an unhealthy influence on Amanda, or was he just looking for trouble? He hadn't kept tabs on Amanda's friends before, and look what had happened. He wished he knew how to find out about this girl without divulging his fears concerning his daughter's behavior. Would it be so awful to tell someone that he needed help? Maybe he had to talk to Sam, no matter how embarrassing or how difficult it was.

"Daddy, there's Maria." Kelsey pointed toward a table near the deck.

Grady glanced in that direction. "Looks like her table's full. We'll have to eat somewhere else."

"But, Dad—"

"No but's. It's not like you don't see her every day."

"But I don't see her every day."

"Well, almost."

"If I can't eat with her, I want to sit with her during outdoor church, okay?"

"Okay," he replied, wondering whether that meant he had to sit with her, too. He wasn't prepared to do that any more than he was prepared to worship. He wanted to escape.

"Have you ever been to outdoor church?" Kelsey asked as they found seats at a table near the outer edges of the yard.

"No."

"I think it's going to be cool. Gramma Reynolds never took us to outdoor church. Are you going to take us to church now that we live here?"

That was about the last question he wanted to hear. This was getting more and more complicated. Why did Kelsey have to ask so many questions?

"Maybe you can go with Maria."

"Dad, don't you believe in God?"

Grady stared at his daughter. Now she *really had* asked the last question he wanted to hear. "You know, Kels, that's something I'm working on."

"Well, *I* believe in God." She waved her pink-cast-clad arm in the air. "He made everything."

Such childlike belief. She hadn't had to live through the disappointments of life yet. Or had she? She had lost a mother. But a mother she barely remembered. It wasn't the same as his loss. Nor did it carry the hurt or the guilt that it did for him.

"I guess you're right. Is that what you learned when you went to church with Gramma Reynolds?" Grady asked, not wanting to disagree with Kelsey's assessment.

She nodded. "That's what I learned in Sunday school. Can I go to Sunday school here?"

"We'll see. Now, eat your breakfast." He hoped she wouldn't ask any more questions, especially about religion. He didn't want to look bad in the innocent eyes of his child.

After most folks had finished eating, a group of men started to arrange chairs in a big semicircle with a center aisle in preparation for the worship service. A group of musicians set up instruments on the deck, while several people tested the sound system. Grady joined in the group that helped clear away the food and the grills, pots and pans that the workers had used for breakfast. He tried not to think about the upcoming worship service. Thinking about it just made his stomach churn.

When Sam rang his cowbell, people found seats and the musicians began to play. Now Grady faced a decision. He could either sit with Kelsey or leave her with Maria and wander toward the back, where he could watch from a distance and not have to participate. If he was honest with himself, maybe he had to admit he had always been at a distance from God. He had been too busy with his career to attend church on a regular basis. Nina had done that with the girls. And he'd seen where that had led.

To nothing good.

"Let's go sit with Maria. She's sitting in the third row." Without waiting for him, Kelsey skipped toward the front. When she realized he hadn't followed, she turned and looked at him. "Dad, come on."

"You go ahead. I'm going to talk to Amanda. I'll be there later."

Kelsey hurried on without a backward glance. He was glad that she wanted him to be with her, but he was also glad that she was independent enough to go without him. He surveyed the area until he saw Amanda. She sat at the back with Courtney and a couple of other teens who lived at the children's home. Why had Amanda picked them as friends? Did she feel more comfortable with kids who had been in trouble than with kids who did the right things? Could he find out? The questions continued to plague him.

Grady leaned against a tree in the woods at the edge of the yard. Maybe he could stand here and observe Amanda and gain some answers. At least this would give him an excuse not to sit up front with Kelsey and Maria.

How would that fly with Kelsey? Amanda was beyond that stage when a child thought a parent was wonderful and could do just about anything, but Kelsey still looked up to him. He couldn't disappoint her. Torn between sharing time with his younger daughter and not wanting to be a hypocrite, he stood rooted to the ground as surely as the tree he rested against.

He continued to watch Amanda. She and Courtney leaned close together as they talked. He would love to know the subject of their conversation. What did teen girls discuss? Boys? Yeah. Boys. How was he ever going to talk to Amanda about that?

Worry wove its way around his every thought. No matter where his mind took him, something triggered anxiety. Amanda. Kelsey. Maria. Work. Soon his brain would be a pretzel of twisted thinking.

While Grady let his mind roam over his worries, a familiar-looking man with dark brown hair and a slight build strolled over. He extended his hand. "Hi, I'm Derek Hunter. We met at Sammy's birthday party. My wife, Suzi, and I are houseparents here."

"Oh, yes. I remember. Good to see you again."

"Your daughter has a wonderful singing voice."

"Thanks. She didn't get her talent from me," Grady said with a chuckle, wondering whether this man had a reason for seeking him out or was just being friendly. Folks here went out of their way to make him feel welcome.

"I noticed your daughter has befriended Courtney, one of the girls who lives in our home. She's been with us since early in the summer and she's had some difficulty fitting in. I just wanted to let you know that it's nice to see your daughter making friends with her. Every kid needs a friend."

"I'm glad she can help," Grady said. Should he be worried or proud? Maybe these girls had found companionship because they were both outcasts. Grady didn't want to deal with any more questions, but he couldn't avoid answering them at some point.

"I thought I'd be the only one here." Derek lounged against the tree next to the one Grady leaned on. "I have a bad back and can't sit in those chairs for any length of time."

Grady glanced at Derek and smiled, although he wasn't happy at all. He'd thought he'd have this spot all to himself and not have to participate in the proceedings. If he had to have company, he'd rather sit with Kelsey and Maria. At least he didn't have to explain anything to them. "I'm really sorry I have to leave you back here by yourself, but I promised my younger daughter I would sit with her. I came back here to make sure Amanda was settled before I went up front."

Derek chuckled. "Oh, don't worry about me. I'm just keeping an eye on the kids back here to make sure they behave. You know how they can be sometimes."

"Yeah." Grady nodded. "If Amanda's any problem, please let me know."

"I'm sure they'll be fine, but I like to keep tabs on them."

"It was nice talking to you, Derek." Grady shook hands with him and thought about the promise he had made to himself about keeping better tabs on Amanda. "I'll see you later."

Grady hurried toward the third row, where Kelsey sat next to Maria. Kelsey spied him as he stopped at the end of the row. "Hey, Dad, I saved a seat for you."

"Thanks, sweetheart," he said, eyeing the open seat on the other side of Maria.

Maria looked up at him. "We can move down if you want to sit next to Kelsey."

Whatever. The word hung on the tip of his tongue, but he didn't say it. He really didn't want to sit anywhere, but he didn't want to sound rude. "Okay."

Kelsey jumped up. "Dad, is it okay if I sit on the end and you sit next to Maria?"

"Sure." Grady moved past Kelsey and wondered whether his daughter might be trying to play matchmaker. He mustered a smile and glanced at Maria, just as the song leader greeted the crowd and asked them to stand for an opening prayer. After the prayer, the sound of praises to God rose all around him. He stood, but he didn't sing. He felt out of place. He shouldn't be here, but he was stuck. Too many things stood between him and God. As far as Grady could see, nothing would change that.

As the service progressed, Grady tried not to think about any of it. But when he wasn't concentrating on the service, his mind wandered to the woman sitting next to him. Her sweet soprano voice lifted the words of the praise songs, and he couldn't ignore them. But he didn't want to listen to their message. He hardened his heart against them and the words of Pastor Craig's sermon. He'd worked so hard not to listen that, by the end of the service, he had a supersized headache. After the last song and the closing prayer, he just wanted to get away. But he had nowhere to go.

Folks filed out of the rows of chairs, and he turned as Maria touched his arm. "Pastor Craig gave a wonderful sermon, didn't he?"

Staring at her, Grady considered whether she really wanted an honest answer. She should know that he didn't care about all this religious stuff.

Kelsey tugged on his arm and saved him from having to answer Maria's question. "Dad, will you fix hot dogs for lunch?"

He looked down at his daughter. "You had them last night. Aren't you getting tired of hot dogs?"

"No, I love hot dogs," she said, hardly able to stand still.

"Okay."

"Yippee. I'm going to get them out of the cooler." Kelsey raced away.

"That must make it easy for you to cook—hot dogs every night," Maria said with a laugh.

Grady chuckled and hoped she wouldn't return to her earlier question. "That or pizza."

"I'd go for the pizza. At least you can sneak some veggies on that."

Grady shrugged. "If they don't pick them off. I have to admit, since we've moved here, the girls probably haven't been eating the most nutritional meals. I'm a terrible cook. At least when we lived in California, the nanny cooked them a good meal."

"Are you planning to hire a nanny here?"

"No. There's an after-school program for Kelsey, and Amanda's old enough to stay by herself for a couple of hours. My work schedule here shouldn't keep me away at night."

"That's good."

"I hope so." Did this score any points with Maria? And why did he care? Maybe because the girls liked her so much. Maybe because he was beginning to like her too much, himself.

After lunch people of all ages gathered near the deck while Sam explained the afternoon's activities. Some of the older women had games and crafts for the younger children. Other activities included volleyball, badminton or croquet. A number of adults organized a coed softball game.

When Grady was satisfied that Kelsey was under good supervision and wouldn't do anything to destroy her cast or break her other arm, he joined the softball game. Standing on the sidelines, he waited for his turn at bat.

Jillian approached. "Hey, Grady. Can I talk to you for a minute?"

"Sure. What about?"

Jillian glanced at Beth, who stood on the pitcher's mound. "I see you've discovered your new sister-in-law has a wicked pitch."

Grady threw back his head and laughed. "Yeah. Clay didn't warn me that his wife could throw like that."

"Did he ever tell you about the time she dunked him in the dunking booth with that pitch?"

"No. When did that happen?"

"Last year, at the fall festival. They have one every year at the elementary school to raise funds for something they need." She eyed him. "Maybe they should recruit you for the dunking tank this year. In fact, I think I'll suggest it."

"Is that why you wanted to talk to me?"

Jillian shook her head. "No, I wanted to talk to you about Amanda."

Grady's stomach sank. Was Amanda in trouble? "Why?"

"Do you think she would sing at the grand-opening ceremony for the assisted-living facility? My mom requested it, and Maria said we can easily fit it into the program."

"Oh, wow! I don't know. She's never sung solo in public, except the other night."

"Would you ask her?"

"I think you should ask. You know how teenagers can be. She might be more responsive to you."

"Then, it's all right with you if she wants to do it?"

"Yeah." Grady shrugged. "But I have no idea what she'll say."

"I'll talk to her. See you later." She turned toward the house.

When his turn came to bat, his mind wasn't on the ball game. It was on Amanda. How would she react to Jillian's request? He hoped his daughter's recent belligerent attitude wouldn't present itself. While he was stewing over Amanda's behavior, he struck out. Was he going to strike out with his daughter, as well? That reminded him that he still should talk to Sam, but he wondered how that would happen when Sam always seemed to be surrounded by a crowd.

After supper folks meandered down to the lake for a campfire. As the sun set behind the stand of trees surrounding the lake, the oranges and reds in the sky reflected in the water. The fire crackled and the flames danced, lighting the night. Most people sat on either the logs arranged in a circle around the fire or on camp chairs they had brought with them. A few brought marshmallows and toasted them in the fire while they waited for the start of the evening program.

Again Grady hung back, not wanting to get too close. Could he manage to stay in the background tonight, or would he find himself in the middle of the crowd again, as he had this morning? He spied Amanda and Courtney sitting together on one of the logs closest to the fire. Surprised, he wondered what had prompted her to sit near the front. Then he noticed the two boys hovering nearby. Boys. That was the attraction. When it came to boys, Amanda had her radar turned on high.

"Hey, Dad. Wanna toast a marshmallow?"

Grady turned to find Kelsey holding out a couple of long sticks that sported several marshmallows. Holding a stick of her own, Maria stood next to Kelsey. He really didn't want to toast marshmallows, but this was part of being a better father—doing stuff with his kids. "Sure. Let me have one of those. Do you know how to do this?"

"You don't know how, either?" Kelsey handed him a stick. "Maria said she'd show me how."

Grady walked toward the fire with Kelsey and Maria. "I can't remember ever toasting marshmallows."

Maria chuckled. "You mean, I have two novices here?"

"Guess so." Grady looked at Maria. Her beautiful features glowed in the firelight. Her dark eyes reflected the flames as she looked at him. His emotions ran on so many different levels when it came to Maria. She made him smile. She made him wary. What was he going to do about her?

"You're telling me you're thirty-six years old and you've never toasted marshmallows?" She paused and pretended to think. "Oh, I forgot. You were—"

"Don't tell me I didn't know how to have fun."

"I didn't say that. You said it for me."

"You'd better be careful. I have a stick here."

"So do I." She took a fencer's stance. "Are you challenging me to a duel?"

"Daddy, you're going to ruin the marshmallows."

Laughing, Grady put an arm around Kelsey's shoulders and gave her a hug. "We're just kidding."

"I know, but you still could've ruined them." Kelsey made a face at him.

"Okay, you two, let me show you how this is done." Maria held her stick just above the flames and slowly rotated it. "The trick is to get the marshmallows golden brown without catching them on fire." She pulled her stick from the fire and held it up. "See?"

Grady grinned at her. "But what if I like mine burnt?"

"Then, burn them." Grimacing, she shook her head. "Yuck."

Grady stuck his marshmallows into the fire and moments later brought them out blazing. Then he blew out the flames. Three charred blobs clung to the stick. "Take a look at these. This is how I like them."

"Let me see you eat them," Kelsey said, wrinkling her nose. "I like mine and Maria's better."

"Good. Then you won't eat mine." Grady plucked the scorched mess from the stick and popped it into his mouth. Basically burned sugar. He wouldn't give them any hint that it tasted awful. He swallowed then smiled. "Tasty."

Maria looked at him, skepticism written on her face. "You really don't sound that sincere."

Unable to contain himself, Grady laughed. "Okay, you found me out. They were overdone."

"Would you like to try one of mine?" Maria asked, taking a marshmallow off her stick.

"Sure."

"Open wide."

Grady did as he was instructed, and Maria placed a warm, sticky marshmallow in his mouth. Then she ate the remaining marshmallows herself. He let the confection melt on his tongue while he watched her lick her lips. He couldn't look away. The thought of kissing those lips stuck in his brain. She had him mesmerized and that would only lead to problems.

Her gaze slid to his, and he swallowed a lump in his throat that he hadn't realized was there. He was glad she couldn't read his mind. He knew he was asking for big trouble if he let thoughts of kissing Maria linger.

"Dad, they're getting ready to start. We gotta sit down."

Thankful for the intrusion, Grady glanced down at Kelsey, who still had one marshmallow left on her stick. "Eat your marshmallow, then we'll sit down."

As Kelsey claimed a spot on one of the logs near the fire, Grady saw no way to escape to the back. He was stuck in the front and would have to deal with it, even if it gave him a headache.

While Grady prepared to block the proceedings from his mind, Sam greeted the gathering. A group of teens stood off to the side. Then Grady noticed that Amanda was among them.

Stepping to the front, Sam motioned for the teens to join him. "We are in for a treat this evening. Some of the kids practiced together this afternoon and are going to perform a few skits for us." Sam stepped aside as the members of the group took their positions.

Grady watched Amanda with a growing sense that he didn't know his daughter at all. How had she gone from a sullen, unhappy girl to this bubbly young woman he saw performing in front of all of these people? Laughter filtered through the audience as the skit unfolded. Grady had had no idea his older daughter liked to act, as well as sing. This weekend had revealed a lot about her and made him realize he needed to spend more time with his children. Despite the humorous bent to the story, it carried a message about putting trust in God—something Grady still couldn't swallow.

Following the skits and the singing, people continued to mill around the campfire. Grady scanned the area for Sam and hoped he would have time to talk. Grady wanted to make sense of Amanda's behavior. One minute she was a surly teen, the next a composed young woman who could perform in front of an audience. He wondered what to make of it. Did her friendship with Courtney have something to do with it? Or was his daughter's whole new attitude just a ruse to throw him off guard?

Finally, seeing Sam headed for the house alone, Grady raced in that direction. His heart pounded from the sprint and the thought of asking for Sam's advice about Amanda. But it had to be done.

"Hey, Sam, wait up!" Grady called.

Sam stopped and turned just as he reached the steps going up to the deck. "Grady, what can I do for you?"

Grady took a deep breath and let it out slowly. "Um…I'd like to talk to you privately. Do you have a minute?"

"Sure. Follow me. We can talk in my office." Sam headed in the direction of a small cedar-sided building near the house.

Trying to think of a good way to bring up the problems with Amanda, Grady followed in silence. Was this a good idea at all? Oh, well, he had taken this step now. He had to follow through.

Sam flipped on the light as he entered the building. "Have a seat. What did you want to talk about?"

Grady hesitated, taking in the computer on one corner of the oak desk that dominated the room. This wasn't going to be easy. Finally, he sat on an upholstered wingback chair near a bookcase overflowing with books. "I was hoping you could help me with Amanda."

"Amanda?" Sam gave Grady a curious glance as he sat on a matching chair on the other side of the bookcase.

"Yes, I thought since you counsel kids, you might be able to give me some advice. Clay suggested it."

"I can't guarantee I'll be able to answer your questions, but I'll do my best. Tell me what's troubling you."

Grady contemplated his approach. Did he start out by explaining the situation with Amanda back in California, or should he ask about Courtney? Better to start with Amanda. He took another deep breath and rushed into an account of how he'd found the vodka in Amanda's room. After he finished, he gazed at Sam. "Should I believe her?"

"Do you?"

Grady shrugged. "I just don't know. I want to believe her. But even if she's telling the truth, she was hanging out with the wrong kids."

"But you've moved, so that should help."

"Yes, but I was wondering about the new kids she's befriended." Grady rubbed the back of his neck and gazed at the braided oval rug on the floor. "What can you tell me about Courtney, the girl who lives in one of the homes here?"

"Is she one of Amanda's new friends?"

"Yes." Grady returned his gaze to Sam. "I know you mentioned that some of the kids who come here have had problems with substance abuse. I was just wondering…wondering…"

"Wondering about Courtney?"

"Yes. I thought Amanda might seek out the same kind of friends. I don't want her to get into trouble."

"I can't divulge the reason that Courtney is here, but if you pay close attention to Amanda, her friendship with Courtney shouldn't be a problem."

"You're sure?"

"I can't be completely sure about anything, but I know it would be good for Amanda—and Kelsey, as well—to be part of the church youth group. I've already mentioned getting them involved in the program we do each year after Thanksgiving."

Sam's suggestion made Grady cringe inside. He was slowly being sucked into a situation he wasn't comfortable with. "We'll see."

While they walked back to the camping area, Grady speculated about Amanda's interest in the youth group. He shouldn't stand in her way, because he wanted his girls to be happy. But could he deal with this church business? He didn't want to be a hypocrite.

Maybe if he had been more in tune with God, more involved in church with Nina, she would be alive today, their marriage still intact. He just didn't know anymore. A huge ache welled up inside him. He wanted something to take it away. Was that something God?

Chapter Ten

Maria joined the adults and youngsters hanging around the campfire. When she turned around, she realized Grady had left the campfire. She searched the area but didn't see him anywhere. She looked at Kelsey, who didn't seem concerned that her father wasn't there. She was too busy toasting more marshmallows and using them to make s'mores. Amanda was laughing and talking with a group of teenagers that even included Lauren, who had been reluctant to spend time with Amanda at Sammy's birthday party. Had the tide turned with Amanda? Maria hoped so, for Grady's sake.

While Maria watched, she felt a touch on her arm. She turned. "Hey, Jillian. I know you've got to be excited about how well everything's going this weekend."

"Absolutely. Sam's so pleased with the progress we've made." Jillian looked in the direction of the teens, still laughing and talking near the fire. "I've talked with Grady and told him about Mom wanting Amanda to sing at the grand opening. He said we should ask her. I was hoping you'd do it, since you know her a little bit better than I do."

"Not that much." Remembering how confrontational Amanda had been at times, Maria wasn't sure how the girl would respond. "I suppose I can give it a try."

"Good. Let's go talk with her."

Maria followed Jillian over to the group of teens. With apprehension swirling through her brain, Maria waited for an opportunity to approach Amanda. The girl suddenly looked Maria's way. Maria smiled and motioned for Amanda to come over. Surprisingly, she came without hesitating.

"Hi, have you seen my dad?"

"No." Maria glanced at Jillian. "Have you seen him?"

Jillian nodded. "I saw him earlier, talking with Sam, but I don't know where they went."

Amanda returned her gaze to Maria. "What did you want?"

Relief at Amanda's agreeable response gave Maria hope that the girl would be amenable to her request. Despite the girl's demeanor, Maria still hesitated as she turned the phrasing of the question over in her mind. "Jillian and I have been talking about the opening ceremony for the center and we're wondering whether you'd be willing to sing. You have such a lovely voice."

Amanda looked down, but not before Maria caught the beginning of a smile. The teen shrugged and dug the toe of her sneaker into the dusty ground. "What kind of a song?"

"Jillian wants you to sing one of her mom's favorites."

"What is it?" Amanda appeared more her age now, her former pout gone. In its place was an expression of uncertainty.

Jillian stepped forward. "Do you know 'You Raise Me Up'?"

"Yes, but…" Amanda gave Maria a nervous glance. "I—I don't usually sing solos. I just did that last night because it looked like fun. I don't know if I could actually sing for real in front of a big crowd. I might mess up."

Jillian put a hand on Amanda's shoulder. "Why don't I get the music for that song, and you could practice with the karaoke machine? Then, after you've practiced, you can decide whether you're comfortable performing it. Okay?"

"I guess." A smile lingered at the corners of her mouth and her green eyes sparkled with interest. "Maybe I should see what my dad thinks."

"Good idea." Maria could hardly believe this was the same child who, just days ago, had been so hostile to anything her father said. Maybe deep down inside she really cared what he thought.

"There he is." Amanda pointed toward the house.

Maria turned. A strange sensation shimmered through her when her gaze met Grady's. She glanced away, fearing that he might sense her reaction to his presence. Trying to cover her agitation, she turned to Amanda. "You can talk to him now."

Amanda scurried toward her father, not in Kelseylike exuberance but with an eagerness that belied her earlier antagonism. "Dad, come talk to Jillian."

Grady grinned as he looked down at Amanda and put an arm around her shoulders as he fell into step beside her. "Is this about singing for the church program and the grand opening?"

"Yeah, how did you know about the opening?" Amanda stepped out of his embrace, and a little frown creased her brow.

Maria held her breath. Was all the goodwill going to

go up in flames like the nearby campfire? Amanda was probably disappointed that singing for the opening wasn't news to her dad. Maybe she had wanted to surprise him.

"Jillian told me earlier, but I wanted to let you make the decision without my interference. Was that okay?"

"Then, you don't mind?"

"Of course not. I didn't know you could sing like that."

"That's because you never came to any of my school choir concerts. You were always working."

Amanda's tone wasn't angry or even accusatory, but Maria could tell by Grady's expression that the words cut him to the heart. He hung his head, but quickly looked up. "I know, but I hope that won't happen anymore. And I hope you'll sing for the opening, because I think you'll do a wonderful job."

"Thanks." Amanda hugged Grady. "The church program will be fun, and Jillian's going to help me practice for the opening."

Amanda's reaction astonished Maria. The change in the girl was amazing. Her choice to get involved in the youth program probably stemmed from a need to find friends. Maybe her earlier attitude had been a cover for feeling as though she didn't fit in. Now she had a place to belong and, hopefully, that would make life easier for Grady. And he was actually letting Amanda get involved in a church function, when he had so adamantly insisted that his girls didn't need that. What had changed his mind?

Kelsey came crashing into the circle, holding out a graham cracker oozing with marshmallow and chocolate. "Hey, Dad, want a s'more?"

"That looks nasty," Amanda said, making a face. "Gross."

"It's not gross. It's good." Kelsey stuck her tongue out at her sister.

"All right, you two. Quit bickering." Grady reached for the s'more. "Thanks, Kelsey."

"See, Dad likes it." Kelsey taunted Amanda with another face.

"That's enough." Grady's warning made Kelsey clamp her mouth shut, but she still stared at Amanda with narrowed eyes.

Everything was back to normal. The sisters were quarreling again. Up until that point, the discussion between Amanda and Grady had seemed surreal. Too peaceful. Too agreeable. And too good to be true.

"Well, I think we'd better turn in for the night," Grady said, looking at his daughters.

"Aw, Dad. Do we have to?" Amanda whined.

"Yes. Get moving."

"Oh, all right." Amanda made another face at Kelsey when Grady wasn't looking.

Kelsey ignored her and came over to Maria. "Are you going to bed, too?"

"Sure. It's getting late. Morning will be here before we know it." Maria joined Grady and the girls as they headed back to their tents.

The foursome strolled in silence as a chorus of crickets serenaded them. Stars twinkled in the darkened sky and the clean, fresh scent of pine filled the cool night air. But even the beauty and wonder of God's creation didn't create peace in Maria's thoughts because Grady was on her mind.

His presence had kept her off kilter all day. All weekend. Whenever he was near, she had a hard time thinking straight. The way he had been with Amanda and Kelsey the last couple of days painted a completely different picture of the man. He didn't seem to be the same person she had known in California. There wasn't a trace of the man who had called her out at Nina's funeral. Was the change real or just temporary? The doubts and questions continued to plague her. And why was she concerned, anyway?

The answer.

She was beginning to like him too much.

It was more than just the initial attraction to a handsome man she had felt that first day at the office. She respected the Grady Reynolds who managed to make everything go smoothly at work. She liked the Grady Reynolds who had joked with Clay about being a stuffy kid. And she adored the Grady Reynolds who had eaten burned marshmallows and then laughed when he had to admit they tasted awful. All those images of him roamed through her mind and settled in her heart.

But she couldn't let that happen. Even if he continued to be the world's best father and the foundation's best employee, he still had abandoned his faith. She couldn't let herself fall for a man who couldn't share that very important part of her life. Not to mention his ready-made family. As much as she felt drawn to Amanda and Kelsey, Maria just didn't know whether she would have the patience to deal with them on a day-to-day basis.

With only a flashlight to guide the way, Maria glanced at Grady as he walked on the other side of Kelsey. As they neared the tents, Maria kept thinking about the surprise and pride on his face when he'd seen Amanda in the youth skit. And she remembered the rigid set of his shoulders as he'd sat there without participating in the singing that followed. His body language and lack of involvement made Maria sad. Sad for Grady. Sad for his children. And sad for herself that she couldn't help him realize the need for God in his life.

Bright sunshine warmed a beautiful September afternoon as Maria surveyed the crowd gathered to celebrate the opening of the assisted-living facility. She stood on the walkway at the entrance, a jittery sensation filling her chest and dropping into her stomach. She hoped everything would run smoothly as dignitaries began to take their places near the front door.

A portable lectern stood beside a wide red ribbon stretching across the walkway leading to the front doors. The ribbon cutting was just minutes away. Newspaper and television reporters from Spokane and one from the local newspaper, gathered nearby, ready to record the ceremony with notepads and cameras.

Conversation buzzed through the crowd. Quiet settled around them when Grady escorted Jillian and her mother, Eileen Rodgers, up the walkway to the lectern. Jillian and her mother stood off to the side while Grady addressed the crowd. He thanked them for coming, then introduced Jillian. When he stepped away, he smiled at Maria, almost as if he was seeking her approval.

Maria tried to keep her attention on Jillian as she praised the community for their support and explained the reasons behind the development of the facility. But her gaze kept drifting to Grady. She didn't want to think about the way his navy blue suit showed off his broad shoulders or the way his smile made her stomach flip-flop.

While she stood there, someone tugged on the sleeve of her suit jacket. She looked down. Kelsey grinned up at her. "Hi," she whispered.

Maria put a finger to her lips, and Kelsey gave her an impish grin. Maria put an arm around Kelsey's shoulders and pulled her close. Since Labor Day, she had spent most evenings with Grady's girls while he worked late to get things ready for the opening. She had also helped Amanda practice singing with the audio equipment at the facility. During that time Maria had become more involved in Amanda's life than she had ever dreamed. The biggest surprise had come when the teen had talked about her fears and worries and sought Maria's advice. Even when Grady was home, Amanda would often pop up to Maria's apartment, just to talk about her day.

Both girls had wormed their way into Maria's life. She had become too attached to the lovable but quarrelsome sisters. Soon, her house would be finished and she would move, leaving them behind. The thought saddened her, but she chased it away. She tried to tell herself that these girls weren't her concern and neither was their workaholic father. His behavior during Labor Day weekend had fooled her into thinking he had changed. He could be charming and attentive, but it never lasted. She tried to pound that point home every time she looked his way.

Applause erupted around her. Belatedly, she joined in, hoping no one had noticed she wasn't paying attention. She glanced down at Kelsey, who had squirmed away to get a better look as Grady, Jillian and Eileen took a huge pair of scissors and approached the ribbon.

Camera shutters clicked and more applause filled the air as the threesome wielded the scissors. The ribbon split in two and floated to the ground.

Grady opened the door for Jillian and Eileen. They walked inside, followed by the rest of the crowd. The smell of new construction still lingered in the large gathering room just past the reception area. Folding chairs set in orderly rows filled the room. Guests began filing in as Jillian, Eileen, Grady and the dignitaries took their seats on the raised platform. With Kelsey and Amanda following, Maria hurried to the reserved section in the front row.

After the crowd quieted, Grady introduced the mayor of Pinecrest. He gave a speech followed by a few words from other dignitaries. The whole time Maria tried not to stare at Grady, but her gaze was drawn to him time after time as he listened intently to the speakers.

Finally, Jillian stepped to the podium and motioned for her mother to join her. "I want to thank everyone again for coming today to share this momentous day with us. My mother would like to say a few words."

Jillian stepped aside, and Eileen came to the microphone. She unfolded a paper and spread it out on the podium. Her soft voice carried over the microphone as she spoke. "I also want to thank everyone for joining us today. I'm going to introduce Amanda Reynolds, who is going to sing 'You Raise Me Up' for us. I chose this song because my family, my church and this community have continued to raise me up as I face an uncertain future. Thank you so much. Please enjoy the song."

Eileen and Jillian returned to their seats as Amanda made her way onto the stage. Maria gave Amanda a thumbs-up sign as she took the microphone out of its holder. A little smile curving her mouth, she stepped in front of the podium. Someone cued the music and the intro to the song played over the sound system. Just as had the night she'd done the karaoke, Amanda's strong clear voice rang through the gathering room.

Maria couldn't miss the pride on Grady's face while he listened to his daughter. Taking in the meaning of the words, Maria felt a lump rise in her throat. She closed her eyes against the tears that threatened. She couldn't get all weepy here in a crowd. When she opened her eyes again, she blinked furiously to gain control. As Amanda sang the last chorus, Maria didn't dare look at Grady. If she did, the tears would surely come.

Just at that moment, a small hand slipped into Maria's. She glanced down at Kelsey, who was enthralled by her sister's performance and seemingly unaware that she had grabbed Maria's hand. Maria felt as if she would burst with love.

Why was it, after she had fully convinced herself that she couldn't have a satisfying relationship with a workaholic man or deal with a ready-made family, that Grady and his girls continued to impact her life? They called to her just like the song. Called to her to be more than she could be. She tried to erase the thoughts from her mind, but they wouldn't go away. They seemed to resurrect themselves over and over again, like the annoying pop-ups on her computer.

She should pray about this situation, but she feared that God was asking her to do something she just wasn't ready to do. She'd answered the call to spend two years helping with her brother's family while his wife fought cancer. She'd spent a year on the mission field. She had never said no.

Maria dreamed of a family of her own when the right time came. She wanted to be alone with a new husband—a man who put his family first. And yet here she was, drawn to everything she didn't want.

Loud applause shook her from her thoughts. Amanda's face beamed as she took a little bow. Eileen hugged the girl. Then Jillian and Grady took turns giving Amanda a hug. Her smile grew wider. Maria's heart grew fuller—filled with affection for Amanda and Kelsey *and* their dad.

Still holding Maria's hand, Kelsey gazed up at Maria and whispered, "She did really good, didn't she?"

Smiling, Maria leaned over and whispered, "She did great."

Kelsey smiled. The sight reminded Maria that, despite the two girls' disagreements, deep down they still loved each other. Loving someone meant being able to get past the bad times. That was what love was all about—taking the good with the bad. That was why her attraction to Grady couldn't grow into anything else. She couldn't overlook the bad.

While those troubling thoughts ran through Maria's mind, the ceremony ended. Jillian invited all the attendees to enjoy refreshments and take a tour of the facility. Soon the hum of conversation sounded throughout the gathering room. After Maria congratulated Amanda on her performance, the girls hurried off to be with Grady. Maria hung back, afraid to be engulfed in their family circle. Throughout the rest of the day's activities, she managed to avoid any prolonged contact with them.

After today she and Grady would have only minimal

dealings at work. He had moved his office into this building while she remained at the foundation headquarters out on the edge of town. It was better this way. The less time she spent with Grady and his girls, the less chance there would be to grow more involved in their lives. This was the way she wanted it. She was sure of it.

Absolutely sure.

Maybe if she said it enough times, she would really believe it.

Chapter Eleven

Rain pelted Maria's umbrella as she dashed from her car to her apartment. The week following the grand opening had brought cooler temperatures and rain—something they didn't need for tonight's football game. Unlocking her door, she glanced at the sky and hoped the weather would change. Once inside, she glanced in the mirror and fluffed her hair with her hand in an attempt to brush out the raindrops that had blown in under the umbrella.

While she was shrugging out of her jacket, the phone rang. Her pulse hammered when she heard Grady's voice. "How's it going?" he asked, his voice carrying an uncertain tone.

"Fine. I just got home."

"I'm glad I caught you."

The phone line grew silent, and Maria wondered why he was calling and why he seemed so hesitant. "I'm surprised to hear from you."

"I—I have a favor to ask you."

"What's that?"

"Could you check on Amanda and Kelsey?" He didn't pause to let her answer, but rushed into the next sentence. "I have reports to do before I go home. I promised the girls I'd take them to the high-school football game tonight. There's no way I'll finish in time. Do you mind taking them?"

"Do you think they'll want to go in this rain?"

There was silence again. "It's raining?"

"Yes." She tamped down her anger as her stomach plummeted. He was so involved in his work that he didn't even realize it was raining.

"I've been buried in these reports and haven't even looked out the window." Papers rustled in the background. "I doubt they'll want to go if the weather's bad. Would you still look in on them? I want to make sure they aren't trying to kill each other." He laughed halfheartedly.

"Yeah, sure. Did you have plans for supper?" Maria sighed inwardly as she waited for his response. He was working late. Same old story, new version.

"We were going to eat at the game. Um…you and the girls can decide what you want to do."

"Okay. What time do you expect to get home?" Maria wanted to give Grady a piece of her mind about falling back into his previous patterns, but she held her tongue. It wasn't her business. Or was it? She hated the thought that she might be enabling him in his workaholic behavior, but she couldn't abandon Amanda and Kelsey. They needed supervision.

"I'm not sure how long I'll be. I'll give you a call when I know more. I really appreciate this. Thanks."

"No problem," she replied, although she had the urge to slam the phone down. "I'll talk to you later."

After she changed clothes, she grabbed her jacket and headed downstairs to see how Amanda and Kelsey were doing. She knocked on the back door.

Kelsey opened the door. "Hi, Maria. Dad called and said you'd be coming down." Kelsey grabbed Maria's hand and pulled her into the kitchen. "I'm so glad you're going to be here."

Despite her annoyance with Grady, Kelsey's greeting chased away Maria's discontent. "Me, too. Where's Amanda?"

"Right here." Amanda appeared in the doorway between the kitchen and the dining room. Her old sullen expression made it clear how she felt about her father's no-show. "So, now what are we going to do?"

"Dad said we could decide," Kelsey said with her usual exuberance. "I think we should order pizza."

Amanda gave Kelsey a venomous look. "I thought we were going to eat at the game."

"I don't want to go to the game in the rain. I'll get my cast wet." Kelsey made a face at Amanda. "Besides, I thought you said football was lame."

"I don't care about the game. I just wanted to be with my friends." Shaking her head, Amanda rolled her eyes. "You and your dumb cast. Put a plastic bag on it."

Maria didn't want to sit in the rain to watch a football game, but she didn't want to appear to take sides. "We have a couple of hours. Let's wait and see what the weather looks like at game time."

"Okay." Amanda grimaced, then turned and retraced her steps. "I'm going back to my room."

"Do you have homework?" Maria called after her.

Amanda stopped and turned. "What's it to you?"

Maria eyed Amanda and decided not to let her get

away with her rude comeback. "That isn't the way to answer me. I expect you to treat me with respect. I asked about the homework so you could get that out of the way if you had some."

"Well, I don't. I'm sorry." She turned and didn't look back as she disappeared into the bedroom.

The girl who had sung so beautifully and confided in Maria that she wanted to attend church had disappeared. The belligerent teenager had returned, but at least she had said she was sorry.

Maria didn't know how to deal with Amanda's attitude or how to ease the tension. How much of the girl's mind-set had to do with Grady's absence? The situation reminded her too much of her own childhood. She hadn't dealt well with her own father's absence, and she wasn't doing much to help Amanda with her father's.

"I don't have homework, either. My teacher usually doesn't give homework on weekends," Kelsey announced with a big smile. "What should we do?"

No matter how much time Maria spent with Amanda and Kelsey, she could never get over the difference between the two girls. Kelsey usually took things in stride while Amanda let every little thing throw her. "Is there something you had in mind?"

"Let's play a game."

"What?"

Kelsey ran into the laundry room off the kitchen and rummaged through a cupboard next to the dryer. She returned carrying a battered box. "We can play Sorry! My gramma Reynolds used to play with me."

"Okay." Maria settled at the kitchen table as Kelsey got the game board out.

In a few minutes they were deeply engrossed in the game as they moved their pieces around the board. They laughed and joked while they enjoyed the competition.

"What's so funny?"

Maria glanced up to see Amanda standing in the doorway. "Kelsey keeps bumping me back. Every time I get out, she comes along and sends me back. I'm making no progress."

"I'm winning! I'm winning!" Kelsey smiled and bounced in her seat.

"Don't get too confident. That game can turn around in a hurry." Amanda sat down at the table. "It stopped raining."

"It did?" Kelsey hopped up and looked out the window in the back door. Then she turned to Maria. "Can we go to the game?"

"If that's what you want to do. Let's take a look at the radar to see if there's any more rain headed this way. We can check on my computer."

"Okay." Apparently having forgotten the game she was winning, Kelsey headed out the door without waiting for Maria.

Maria glanced at Amanda. "Do you want to come or stay here?"

"I'll go with you."

The threesome went up to Maria's apartment, and she turned on her computer and checked the weather. "Looks like the rain's gone. So we can go to the game."

"Yippee!" Kelsey jumped up and down. "Can we go now?"

Maria glanced at the clock. "The game starts in forty-five minutes. We'll leave as soon as you get your jackets, and we'll take an umbrella just to be safe."

* * *

After they arrived at the football field, they bought hot dogs and found seats on the bleachers.

"There's Courtney." Amanda pointed to a group of kids sitting a couple of rows down. "May I go sit with her?"

"Yes, but stay there when the game is over so I know where to find you," Maria replied, noticing that Courtney's houseparents were sitting in the same row. Despite the presence of the houseparents, Maria was thankful that Amanda had asked permission instead of just taking off.

"Thanks. I will." Amanda scurried down the bleachers and settled in with her friends.

Moments later Maria spied Clay, Beth, Jillian and Sam as they made their way into the stands. When they saw Maria and Kelsey, they waved.

"Got room for us up there?" Jillian called.

"Sure." Maria motioned for them to come up.

Minutes later the band played the national anthem, the teams took their places on the field and the game began. It had been a long time since Maria had attended a high-school football game. The cheering crowd, the band, the cheerleaders and the school colors were all part of the pageantry and excitement.

"There's Max!" Kelsey yelled as she pointed at the field.

"How can you tell?" Maria asked.

"He's number eighty-two."

"She's right," Clay said, giving her a high five. "But it probably won't be too long before we can't read anyone's number. That field is muddy from all the rain."

Kelsey clapped her hands. "He's going to score lots of touchdowns."

"I hope you're right." Clay gave her another high five.

With the sights, sounds and smells of the game filtering around her, Maria kept thinking about Grady. He should be here instead of working. She had to quit thinking about him, but being with his girls kept him front and center in her mind. Suddenly, the people in the stands were on their feet.

Kelsey was jumping up and down and tugging on Maria's arm. "What's happening? I can't see!"

Maria glanced at the field. A pile of muddy players lay on the ground near the goal line. She looked down at Kelsey. "Pinecrest almost scored a touchdown. Stand on the bench. Then you can see."

Kelsey hopped up just in time to see Max catch a pass and run into the end zone to score. Screaming and shouting, she jumped up and down. "Max scored, just like I said!"

Everyone in the row was laughing, cheering and giving each other high fives. Maria noticed that even Amanda was on her feet, cheering with her friends. Now, if only Grady could be here to share it with his kids. *Quit thinking about him.*

Someday, years from now, he'd regret not spending more time with them. It wasn't her worry. So why did she keep thinking about it? For the rest of the game, Maria tried to concentrate on everything except Grady. Success didn't come easily.

After the game, which Pinecrest won in a rout, Maria said goodbye to the group from church. Then she grabbed Kelsey's hand, and they made their way down the steps to meet Amanda.

"Can we wait to see the team?" Kelsey asked as they

passed the large crowd outside the locker room. "I want to tell Max how I predicted he would score lots."

Amanda rolled her eyes at her. "Like he's gonna care."

"You don't know." Kelsey waved her cast in the air. "He's the one who told the other players to sign my cast."

"Whatever." Amanda rolled her eyes again.

Maria looked at the girls. "We don't have anywhere else to be, so we can wait for a few minutes."

"Goody." Kelsey hurried to find a spot close to the door.

Maria followed and stood a few feet away, keeping an eye on Kelsey. Amanda lounged against the building, an attitude of indifference painted on her face.

Finally, the team appeared to noisy applause. Handshakes, congratulations and cheers came from proud parents and friends as the players filed through the door.

When Kelsey spotted Max, she pushed her way through the throng. Maria wanted to reach out and pull her back, but Max grinned when he saw her. "Hey, squirt, you came to the game."

"Yeah, Maria brought us." Kelsey's eyes grew wide with excitement. "I predicted you would score lots of touchdowns."

Max laughed. "I'll have to make sure you come to every game, so I can score every time."

"That'd be cool."

Maria stepped up beside Kelsey. "I wouldn't be making any plans, Kelsey."

Max winked. "I'll talk to your dad. See what he says."

Maria wondered what Grady would say about Kelsey going to all the games. He might never take the time to go because he was too busy with work. While Maria pondered his possible reaction, she noticed Amanda. She was still standing off to one side, but her gaze was trained on Max's friend Nathan. Maria didn't miss Amanda's look of adoration as she watched him.

Remembering Amanda's fascination with the boys on moving day, Maria considered whether the teen's bluster about not wanting to see the players after the game had all been a ruse. Even though Maria couldn't miss the girl's interest, she still didn't join the group gathered around Max and Nathan. Maria wished she could help, but she doubted Amanda would welcome her advice. Besides, Nathan was probably a little old for Amanda. The girl definitely wouldn't want to hear that.

Maria shook the thoughts away. This wasn't her child. She shouldn't be taking on Amanda's problems. This was Grady's territory. But he was AWOL.

While Maria stewed over the situation, Brittany invited Amanda into the circle. Her face lit up like the lights illuminating the football field. When Amanda joined the group, the bravado she had displayed the day they moved in was missing. A conversation ensued that Maria couldn't hear. Then Amanda turned and surveyed the area until she found Maria.

She darted in Maria's direction. "Is it all right if I go to the youth party at church? Max said he'd bring me home."

Maria's mind whirled. This definitely wasn't her job. She couldn't make this decision. "You have to talk to your dad."

"But he's not here." That familiar sulk crept across Amanda's face. "He's never around when I need him."

Maria couldn't argue with that. "We'll call him." She fished her cell phone out of her purse.

On the third ring Grady answered. Without hesitating, Maria launched into an explanation of the circumstances. For a moment, he didn't respond, and she hoped he wouldn't say no.

Finally, he replied, "I'm glad you called. I was just getting ready to call you."

"Are you finished?"

"No. That's the problem. I don't know when I can leave. The nurses' aide who works the eleven-to-seven shift called in sick. I haven't been able to find anyone to come in for her. I can't leave one nurse here to deal with some of the patients who have to be lifted. One person can't do that. I've called everyone. Either I get no answer or they can't come in."

"Don't you have someone on call?"

"Yes, for nurses, but not aides. I'll have to change that policy immediately."

"I guess so. Maybe the people you've been trying to reach have been at the game. You might be able to get someone in an hour or so."

"I'm going to keep trying. But in the meantime, I need for you to stay with Amanda and Kelsey. Spend the night, if necessary. Can you do that?"

Maria knew what he said was right. He couldn't leave one person alone to deal with the patients that couldn't do for themselves. She couldn't fault him for staying, even though it hurt his girls. She had to say yes. He wasn't working just to be working. This was an emergency. "Sure. No problem. But what about Amanda?"

"Let me talk to her. And thanks. That takes a load off my mind."

"You're welcome." Maria held out the phone to Amanda. "Your dad wants to talk to you."

Maria couldn't read Amanda's reaction to her father's working late. Maybe as long as she got to go to the party it wouldn't bother her. Maria had never gotten used to having her father coming home well after she had gone to bed. But this wasn't the time to be thinking about her past. She needed to think about what was happening now.

After Amanda finished talking, she handed the phone back to Maria and smiled. "Dad says he wants to talk with you again."

Taking the phone, Maria surmised Amanda's smile meant that Grady had agreed to let her go. "Hello."

"Hi again. I told Amanda she could go to the party. Thanks for doing this." His sigh was audible even over the phone. "I'll see you whenever I can get home."

As Maria slipped the phone back into her purse, she felt a tug on her arm. Kelsey stood there looking as though she had just lost her best friend. This couldn't be same kid who seemed to find something to smile about in almost every circumstance. "What's the matter?" Maria asked Kelsey.

"I can't go to the party because I'm too young."

Maria patted her on the back. "That means you and I can find something fun to do. How about that?"

"Like what?" The question came out of Kelsey's mouth in an almost Amandalike whine.

"Well, how about going back to my place?"

"And what can we do there?" Kelsey's resemblance to her sister didn't fade.

"We'll think of something." Maria searched her mind for anything to appease this once-happy child. Maybe she shouldn't be trying to placate Kelsey, at all. Maybe she should just say, *Quit acting like a baby and get over it. Your turn will come when you get to be Amanda's age.* How many times had she heard that when she was growing up? But she reminded herself that Kelsey wasn't her kid. She wanted to get through the evening without any problems, and if that meant making Kelsey happy, she would.

Kelsey tugged on Maria's arm in her usual fashion. "Well, did you think of anything?"

An idea popped into Maria's brain. "Didn't you mention something about baking things for the school festival? How would you like to bake cookies?"

Kelsey wrinkled her nose. "But won't they go bad? The festival isn't for two weeks."

"We'll put them in the freezer. That'll keep them fresh."

"You're sure?"

"Absolutely. You want to bake cookies?"

"Yeah. Let's go!" Kelsey's smile returned and she grabbed Maria's hand and skipped toward the parking lot.

Hurrying to keep up, Maria resisted the urge to skip along as they made their way to the car. When they got back to the house, Kelsey raced up the stairs to Maria's apartment. Once inside, she bounced into the kitchen. "What kind of cookies are we going to make?"

"What's your favorite?"

"Chocolate chip."

"Is that the kind you want to make?"

"Yeah." Jumping up and down, Kelsey clapped her hands. Then she stopped, a thoughtful expression creasing her brow. She held up her arm. "Will I be able to do that with my cast?"

"Your cast won't be a problem. So let's get busy."

Maria started getting the ingredients from her cupboard and said a little prayer of thanks when she discovered she had everything they needed. "Okay, I'm going to let you do most of the work. Start by reading the recipe. Then tell me what you need to do first."

Kelsey looked over the recipe on the package of chocolate chips then looked up at Maria. "I need to preheat the oven."

"Good. Let me show you how."

For the next hour, Maria guided Kelsey through the fine art of making chocolate-chip cookies, including the best part—sampling the cookie dough. After Maria and Kelsey baked the cookies, they washed all the bowls, utensils and cookie sheets and put them away. Then Maria poured two glasses of milk and took a small plate of cookies into the living room. They sat on the couch and enjoyed the tasty products of their labor.

After they finished eating, Maria stood. "Okay, it's time for you to get ready for bed."

"But my dad's not home yet."

"You're going to spend the night with me."

"You mean like a slumber party?"

Maria had visions of laughing and giggling girls talking girl talk and staying up all night. Shaking her head, she laughed. "You and Amanda are going to stay with me tonight, but no slumber party. Since you're here first, you get first choice. You can sleep in the bedroom where I keep my computer, or you can sleep in my room. Amanda will take whatever you don't pick."

Kelsey appeared to be thinking about it. "Where will you sleep?"

"I'll sleep on the pullout bed in the couch."

"Then I'll sleep in your room. But can't I stay up till Amanda gets here?"

Maria glanced at her watch. "By the time you take a

bath and get your pajamas on and I read to you, Amanda will be home."

Maria went downstairs with Kelsey to get her pajamas and her book. When the little girl was ready for bed, they went back to Maria's room. Kelsey climbed into bed. Maria sat on the edge and read to her. As she read, she wondered how this little girl felt about her father's absence. Unlike Amanda, whose feelings were easy to determine, Kelsey didn't show her reaction to the situation.

Just as Maria finished reading, there was a loud knock on the door. She headed for the living room, and Kelsey hopped out of bed and followed. Through the window in the top of the door, Maria saw Max and Amanda. A big smile curved Amanda's lips. That was a good sign.

Maria opened the door. "Hey, did you have a good time?"

"It was okay." Amanda's low-key response belied her smile and the sparkle in her eyes.

"Thanks for bringing her home, Max."

"No problem. Gotta run. I still have to drop Brittany off before I go home."

Without saying much, Amanda went downstairs and got her things and prepared for bed. Maria showed her where she was going to sleep. Amanda said good-night, and Maria closed the door, with Kelsey hovering behind her.

Turning, Maria looked at the younger girl. "Okay, back to bed."

Kelsey scurried to Maria's room and hopped into bed. As Maria tucked her in, she reached up and put her arms around Maria's neck. "Thank you for teaching me how to make cookies and reading to me. I love you."

A big lump rose in Maria's throat. She didn't even mind that Kelsey's cast was digging into her neck. She hugged Kelsey back. "You're welcome. And I love you, too."

Grabbing her own pajamas, Maria blinked back the tears welling up in her eyes. She shut off the light and hurried from the room. Her mind buzzed with thoughts of the evening's events. She didn't feel the least bit sleepy. Instead of getting ready for bed, she went back into the living room and sat on the couch in the dim light coming from the single lamp in the corner of the room.

Maria let her mind wander into dangerous territory. What would it be like to be a part of this family? To be a mother to these girls? They would keep her on her toes. They would exasperate her from time to time. They would enrich her life. But, most of all, there would be love to share. Sometimes having them with her seemed perfect and right. Even Amanda, with her mood swings, had won Maria's affection.

But how did she deal with their father? Her attraction to him was undeniable, but tonight made her temper any thoughts of acting on it. Here was a man who, only weeks ago, had thought she had aided Nina in her betrayal. Yet other images of Grady filled her mind. Him laughing with Amanda and Kelsey while he made pancakes. Him reading to Kelsey. Him taking charge of a project and getting the results he wanted. These were all wonderful and good things that drew her to him.

He was *not* a bad man. He had lots of good qualities that she admired, but she couldn't forget that he was also a man who sometimes didn't have his priorities straight when it came to work, family and faith. She wouldn't want to live the life Nina had lived, never knowing when he would be home. Her mind was running rampant with unlikely scenarios. She shouldn't even consider romance and Grady in the same thought. But she did.

She was twisting herself into knots over a guy who probably didn't have romance on his mind. Was that true? She couldn't help remembering the way he had gazed at her as they stood outside the tents at the camp-out or on the day of the grand opening. Something told her the interest wasn't all on her part. What should she do about it?

Forget Grady Reynolds.

If only it was that easy.

Chapter Twelve

When Grady pulled his car into the garage, a light was still shining in Maria's apartment. Surely, she wasn't still awake at nearly one in the morning. Maybe she had let the girls stay up late. After all, tomorrow wasn't a school day.

He had hoped Amanda and Kelsey would be asleep when he got home, so he wouldn't have to face their disappointment that he hadn't kept his promise. But they had gone to the game, so maybe it didn't bother them at all. He could probably convince himself of that, if he didn't want to face the truth.

He trudged across the yard, the light high atop the pole in the alley illuminating his way. But nothing illuminated his thoughts about how he could face Maria. He had wanted to show her he had changed, but he hadn't. Tonight's scenario, so similar to what had happened just weeks ago, made him feel as though he were in some kind of time warp, forced to repeat the same mistakes week in and week out.

Maria already thought he had been a lousy husband

and now she probably thought he was also a poor father, too. He shouldn't be torturing himself about what she thought. He didn't want another woman in his life that he could disappoint, but there was something about Maria that begged him to disregard all those warning thoughts.

Climbing the stairs, he speculated about how she would greet him. What did it matter? He was tormenting himself for nothing. She didn't have an interest in him. But she absolutely cared about Amanda and Kelsey. That he knew for sure. Over the past few weeks, he had learned that inside her no-nonsense business suit there was a caring heart.

When Grady reached the top of the stairs, he knocked lightly on the door. He waited. No one answered. He listened for voices, but he didn't hear anything. The curtain was drawn over the window in the door. Maybe everyone was asleep, but they had left the light on. He knocked a little harder.

A silhouette appeared on the curtain. "Who's there?" The sweet sound of Maria's voice seemed to take away the chill in the night air and warm his thoughts.

"It's Grady."

The curtains parted, and Maria peeked out. He gave her a little wave, and she opened the door. Sleepy-eyed, she stared at him. "What are you doing here?"

"I finally found someone to come in to cover the shift. Did I wake you?"

She nodded, still not looking completely awake. "I'm sorry. I must've dozed off. I was reading—" She glanced back into the room, where a Bible lay open on the couch. She turned to him again. "I can't believe I fell asleep. Come in."

She stepped aside, and Grady walked in. "I'm the

one who should be sorry for waking you at this hour. I saw the light and thought you must still be up. Where are the girls?"

Maria waved a hand in the direction of the hallway. "They're both sleeping. They can just stay here. I don't mind. You want to peek in on them?"

"Sure." He followed her down the hall.

Maria opened one of the bedroom doors a crack. "Amanda's in here."

A soft beam of light fell across the bed where Amanda slept. She looked so peaceful. His daughter. Part little girl. Part woman. A confusing time for both of them. Grady glanced at Maria and whispered, "Did they have a good time at the game?"

She nodded and closed the door. "And I think Amanda had a good time at the church party, too."

Grady didn't comment as Maria stopped in front of the door at the end of the hallway. He was glad Amanda had had a good time, but he worried that her involvement in church activities would mean his involvement, too.

Maria opened the door and stepped aside. "Kelsey's staying in my room."

Grady glanced at Maria. "You shouldn't have to give up your bed. I can carry Kelsey down to her own room."

"That's okay. I don't mind sleeping on the sofa bed for one night. You don't want to disturb her. She looks comfortable and is sleeping so soundly."

"You call that comfortable?" Grady whispered as he poked his head into the room and motioned toward Kelsey, who lay half uncovered, with one hand slung over her head and the one with the cast hanging over the edge of the bed. "She's my restless sleeper. When she was younger, I had to make sure she didn't tumble out of bed."

Grady inched his way to the bed and gently pulled the covers over his daughter. She stirred but didn't wake up. He backed out of the room and closed the door.

Maria remained silent as she tiptoed back down the hallway while he followed. He wanted to thank Maria, to tell her how much he appreciated her help, but he wasn't sure how to express his gratitude. When she stopped in the living room, he stood there just taking in the wonderful sight of her. She appeared so huggable in her still-sleepy state with her slightly rumpled hair and clothes. He had the urge to pull her into his arms and hold her. He stepped back, fearful that he might act on that urge. He swallowed hard and took a deep breath.

Then he noticed a white streak in her dark hair. He couldn't help reaching out to touch it. "Did watching Amanda and Kelsey turn your hair white?"

"I have white in my hair?"

He nodded. "A big streak. Right here." Still touching her hair, he let his fingers linger on the silken strands. Her lips slightly parted, she gazed up at him. She didn't move. His pulse pounded.

She was standing so close that he could easily take her into his arms and kiss her. The moment the thought crossed his mind, he dropped his hand. He was in more trouble than he had ever imagined. Big trouble.

She turned and looked in the decorative mirror on the wall between the couch and the overstuffed chair. Laughing, she turned and looked at him. "It's flour. I can't believe I didn't notice it before."

"Flour?"

"Yes. Kelsey and I made chocolate-chip cookies for her school's festival bake sale. We put them in the freezer, so they'll keep until the festival."

"When's that?" he asked, thankful that he hadn't acted on his attraction.

"Two weeks from tomorrow."

"Oh, yeah. Beth's trying to get me in that dunking-booth thing." Grady shook his head. "Not something I really want to do."

"You might have fun."

"So you baked cookies after the game?" he asked, trying to avoid more discussion of the dunking booth.

"Yeah," Maria replied, then proceeded to fill him in on the rest of the evening.

"So Amanda had a good time at the party?"

Maria smiled. "I think so. I'm never quite sure with Amanda. She doesn't like to let you know when things suit her. Just when they don't."

Nodding, Grady laughed. "I know. Thanks for helping out tonight."

"I enjoyed it."

"Well, I'd better get going, so you can get back to sleep." And so he could avoid any more temptations to kiss her. "Good night."

"Wait. Let me give you a couple of Kelsey's cookies, so you can tell her how good they are."

"Okay." Afraid that if he followed her into the kitchen he might act on his earlier thoughts, he waited by the door.

When she returned, she handed him a small plastic bag containing two cookies. "They're really good. Kelsey did a good job."

"Thanks." Taking the bag, he made sure their fingers didn't touch. He wasn't sure he could deal with the physical contact right now.

"You're welcome. I guess I'll see you in the morning."

"Yeah. What time should I get the girls?"

"I'll let you know when they're up."

Grady wished there was some way to repay Maria
for her help, but he figured she'd probably be put off
if he offered her money. Should he invite her for
breakfast? With the way he was feeling about her tonight, he wasn't sure spending more time with her
would be good. Maybe he was just tired and so more
susceptible to his attractive coworker. In the morning
he'd be rested and less vulnerable. Or was he kidding
himself? Only one way to find out. "How about joining us in the morning for some pancakes? The girls
would like that."

"I'd love to. Thanks."

"Great. Good night again."

Her bright smile made Grady question the sanity of
the invitation he'd given her. Releasing a harsh breath,
he raced down the stairs without a backward glance. He
had to get away before he did something he would regret.
He reminded himself that he didn't need another woman
in his life. No matter how appealing it might be, any romantic relationship with Maria was out of the question.

The next morning Maria sat at the kitchen table with
Amanda and Kelsey while Grady poured pancake batter
onto the griddle. The batter sizzled and steam curled into
the air. The warm and homey aroma of pancakes mingled with the smell of hot syrup and butter.

"Daddy, make my pancake in the shape of my initial," Kelsey said, bouncing in her seat in her usual exuberant manner. "And do Maria's, too."

Grady smiled at his daughter, then glanced at Maria.
His blue eyes danced with laughter. "Do you want
your initial?"

"Is that your specialty?" Maria asked, trying to ignore the way his attention made her insides sizzle like the pancake batter.

"No, elephant pancakes are my specialty."

"Then, I want an elephant." Maria pressed her lips together as she fought back a smile. She couldn't get over the way Amanda and Kelsey brought out the fun side of their father. He was a different person when his kids made him laugh. *This* Grady Reynolds always managed to appeal to Maria on so many levels. He pulled her in and made her forget the workaholic man who hadn't been there for his wife or his kids in the past.

Even last night when he had peeked in on his sleeping daughters, his concern had touched her. And she couldn't forget the way he had looked at her when he saw the flour in her hair. For just an instant, as he stood so close, she had thought he might kiss her. But then he had jerked his hand away. Just remembering the moment sent little prickles down her spine. Had he invited her to breakfast because he wanted her company, or had he done it to repay her for watching his kids? She wasn't sure she wanted to know the answer.

Kelsey suddenly jumped up, disrupting Maria's thoughts. "I changed my mind. I want an elephant, too."

"All right. Elephants it is." Grady flipped the pancakes that were already on the griddle. "These will be for Amanda and me."

Amanda appeared bored but not sullen as she sat at the table. "That's good, Dad, since I don't think I'm up to eating an elephant this morning."

Kelsey giggled, and Amanda gave her sister a high five. Then the sisters laughed together. Maria couldn't help joining in the laughter, and she didn't miss the way

Grady smiled and gazed at his daughters with unmistakable adoration. *If only he would look at me like that.* The idea inched its way into Maria's thoughts. She shoved it into the basement of her mind, where all crazy notions resided.

Instead of thinking about Grady, Maria focused her interest on Amanda. The girl's wry sense of humor surprised Maria. Too many things about the girl left her dumbfounded. The way her attitudes hopscotched from bored to funny. The way she went from being ostracized to being the center of attention among the church teens. And the way she vacillated between loving and loathing her sister.

Maria was glad to see that Amanda seemed to have overcome her previous problems with the teens from church. Maybe making a few friends was all she had needed to make her life better in this new place. But was the unhappy Amanda lurking somewhere near the surface?

Maria tried to push her thoughts in another direction, but that lent itself to thinking about Grady. She didn't want to do that, either. Despite his late hours last night, his actions this morning showed her that he was trying to be a good father. While she watched him work, her resistance slowly melted like the butter sitting atop the stack of pancakes he had placed in front of Amanda. As she poured the syrup over her pancakes, the phone rang.

Kelsey jumped up. "I'll get it." She raced to the phone.

"Hello." She listened intently for a few moments. Her smile grew wider and her ponytail bounced as she nodded her head. She glanced at her dad and held out the phone. "It's Mr. Lawson. Please say yes."

Grady took the phone, a puzzled expression knitting his eyebrows. "Say yes to what?"

"Just talk to Mr. Lawson," Kelsey replied, barely able to contain her excitement.

As Grady said hello, Maria wondered what Sam had said that had made Kelsey so excited. While Grady listened, she watched the emotions play across his face.

Kelsey tugged on Grady's arm. "Dad, please, please, please say yes."

Grady glanced down at his younger daughter. A near scowl slowly changed to an expression of resignation as he continued his phone conversation. "Sure, that'll be fine."

Kelsey reached out toward the phone. "Daddy, let me talk."

"Okay, we'll see you at three this afternoon." Grady paused and glanced at Kelsey. "Sam, Kelsey wants to tell you something." He gave her the phone.

"Mr. Lawson, is it okay if Maria comes with us? She likes to ride horses, too." Kelsey listened, a smile spreading to her entire face. "Thanks. Bye."

Grady's expression didn't hide his dismay. "Kelsey, you can't go making plans for people. You should've asked Maria, first."

"But, Dad, I want Maria to go with us." The little girl came to Maria's side. "You said you ride horses. You want to go, don't you?" Kelsey's blue eyes petitioned for an affirmative answer.

Maria hesitated. *Yes.* That was what she wanted to say. But Grady's seeming displeasure made her reluctant to accept the invitation. She wanted so much to be a part of their fun day, but she had to admit it wasn't just because Kelsey had asked her. She wanted to push aside all her doubts and spend more time with Grady.

When she was with Grady and his kids, the yearning

for a family life always insinuated itself into her thoughts and shoved aside her carefully constructed goals. Time for herself. Time to do what she pleased. Time without family obligations. That was what she'd thought she wanted. Now she wanted the opposite.

"Hey, I'm sorry Kelsey's trying to coerce you into going with us. Don't feel like you have to." Grady's apology made her decision that much harder.

She smiled, even though little pinpricks of disappointment flitted through her mind because Grady didn't seem to share Kelsey's enthusiasm for her presence. She couldn't kid herself anymore. Despite all the reasons for not getting involved with Grady, she had feelings for this man that had nothing to do with business and everything to do with falling in love. How had she let this happen, with Grady Reynolds, of all people?

She wanted him to care about her and think about her in a romantic sense, not just in association with his children. Sometimes she thought he did, but maybe she had misread the signs. Maybe Jillian had summed up the situation best. He was still grieving. Or maybe he was just afraid of being hurt again.

With all those notions swirling in her mind, Maria pondered her response. "I—I think—"

"I think you should come. Please." Amanda joined Kelsey. "You've got to come. It won't be as fun without you."

Maria's heart warmed at Amanda's insistence. This was so unlike her. No matter what Grady thought, Maria couldn't say no. "Okay, I'll go."

"Yippee!" Kelsey gave Maria an exuberant hug.

As Kelsey stepped away, a look passed between the

girls. Then realization dawned. They were matchmaking. A lump formed in her throat. Swallowing hard, she glanced at Grady. He didn't say another word, but he didn't seem pleased.

What had she gotten herself into?

While Grady drove to Sam and Jillian's place, he tried not to think about the way his daughters had begged Maria to go with them. He knew what they were doing and he didn't know how to put an end to it. He feared they would put too much hope in their attempt at matchmaking and he speculated about whether Maria suspected their motives in asking her. He wondered how he could discourage them, especially when the idea of a relationship with Maria appealed to him, too.

Despite all his promises not to let another woman into his life, Maria had somehow managed to get past the barriers he had erected around his heart. That had become abundantly clear last night, when he had nearly kissed her. And having her share breakfast with them this morning had seemed so right, so natural, something he could get used to every day. But how did Maria feel? She had left little doubt that she thought he had been an absentee husband and father, and last night had probably not helped to change her opinion.

The girls and Maria chattered and didn't seem to notice that he hadn't joined in their conversation. But then, it was mostly girl talk—clothes, school and chick flicks. And they discussed the youth program at church. He didn't miss the fact that both girls expressed an interest in joining the youth activities. Where would that lead? Was he ready to consider his relationship to God and the church again? He scrubbed the thought from his mind as they pulled into the drive that led to Sam and Jillian's house.

Jillian came through the front door to greet them when they emerged from the car. "Hey, good to see you guys. Sam was so relieved that you could come out on short notice when that other group canceled."

"Thanks for inviting us. Kelsey's wanted to do this since we moved here," Grady said, realizing that this invitation had spurred him to do something else he had neglected. "Where's Sam?"

"He's down at the barn. The others are already there and the horses are saddled and ready to go," Jillian replied.

Kelsey ran up to Jillian. "Is Sammy going to go, too?"

Shaking her head, Jillian chuckled. "He's too young for horseback riding. Besides, he's taking a nap. You can see him after your ride."

Kelsey turned. "Can we do that, Dad?"

"Sure. Now, let's get going." Grady motioned toward the barn.

They started down the blacktop road. Kelsey skipped ahead, her hot-pink cast swinging by her side. Sunlight filtered through the pines and scattered shadows on the ground. The fresh scent of the forest surrounded them. The temperatures, hovering near seventy degrees, made a perfect day for horseback riding.

A perfect day for falling in love.

The unexpected thought flitted through his mind like the chickadees flitting through the trees. He tried to shake it away, but it lodged in his mind. Moving the rocks imbedded in the side of the hill would be easier than dislodging the idea from his brain.

With that thought still spinning through his mind, Grady fell into step with Maria. He glanced her way, and she smiled. His pulse danced through his veins like the sunbeams dancing in her dark brown hair. He had to look away. Even then, he had the sudden urge to hold her hand. To avoid acting on the intense impulse, he shoved his hands in his pockets.

He was in deep—deeper than might be good for all of them, especially if Maria didn't share his feelings. Maybe Amanda and Kelsey's presence saved him from doing something he might regret later. Yet, he wasn't worried about what Maria might think today. He wanted to enjoy this time with his girls and with the woman who was slowly changing his mind about what he wanted in life.

When they arrived at the barn, eight adults of varying ages stood in line, ready to take a trail ride. Kelsey could hardly contain her excitement as she grabbed Grady's arm and pulled him toward the line.

Sam waved when he saw them. "Glad to see you made it. We'll have you ready to go in a few minutes."

As the kids from the children's home brought horses from the barn, Sam matched each rider with an appropriate mount.

Grady walked over to Sam and positioned himself so that Kelsey couldn't hear. "Can you give Kelsey a really gentle horse?"

"Actually, I plan to have Kelsey ride with Maria. I don't let younger kids ride by themselves unless they're experienced with horses. And I'll make sure Amanda is riding directly behind me in the line."

Grady smiled, relief settling in his brain. "That's good to know."

Soon everyone was ready. Kelsey protested having to ride with someone until she realized she was being paired with Maria. Kelsey's growing attachment to Maria mirrored his own. With each passing minute, she was becoming more and more a part of his life and his thoughts. That talk he had considered having with his girls earlier now seemed less and less urgent. In fact, it seemed almost unnecessary. But what did he intend to do about his own growing affection for Maria?

While Grady rode directly behind Maria and Kelsey, the question continued to plague him. Maria was not only in his thoughts, she was directly in his line of vision as the horses plodded along the sometimes steep and rocky trail that wound its way through the forest.

He wondered whether he had been so involved in protecting his own feelings that he'd never considered his children's feelings. All their actions and comments made it clear that they missed having a mother. Was he brave enough to put aside his fears and act on his attraction to Maria? The idea of falling in love again and sharing his life with a woman carried all the apprehension, all the possibility of hurt and betrayal associated with Nina and her death. Could he convince Maria that he would make a good husband? Could he convince himself?

The horses made their scripted journey through the forest land that encompassed Sam's house and the other buildings associated with the children's home. The peaceful surroundings did nothing to quell the questions that bombarded Grady while he watched Maria and Kelsey ride just ahead of him. The picture of his daughter sheltered in Maria's arms made pushing away romantic notions of this woman even more difficult.

With a big smile on her face, Kelsey turned and waved several times. Her ponytail bounced as the horse tramped along the trail. And Amanda rode at the front of the line as if she were actually leading the trail ride. Both of his girls were happy. That was what he wanted—their happiness.

He tried not to think about everything that might involve.

An hour later they had completed a route that had taken them up and down hills, through meadowlands and around the small lake on Sam's property. When they arrived back at the barn, the kids who had helped them mount were there to help them dismount.

As soon as Kelsey got off her horse, she came running up to Grady. "Dad, wasn't that just the coolest thing?"

Grady nodded and couldn't help smiling as he put an arm around her and drew her close. "The coolest."

"When can we do it again?" She looked up at him with insistence in her eyes.

"Not until I can walk again."

"Oh, Dad, it wasn't that bad." Kelsey put a hand on one hip.

Amanda joined her sister. "He's just getting old."

Grady laughed. "Okay, you two, don't pick on your old dad that way."

"That's right, girls, don't pick on your father just because he's getting old." Maria winked at the girls, then gave Grady an impish grin.

"You're not picking on me, too, are you?" Slowly shaking his head, Grady let his gaze linger on Maria.

She didn't turn away. "Yes, me, too."

Her words seemed to have an underlying meaning as their gazes held. Or maybe his constant thoughts about her today had him reading more into her statement than she really meant.

"Come on, girls, let's race him to the Lawsons'

house." Kelsey grabbed Maria's hand and ran up the blacktop road.

Amanda joined them. The laughing trio of females soon outdistanced him. As he shuffled along the road after them, he decided maybe he *was* getting old. Time was flying by. His girls were growing up fast. But they seemed happier now than they had in a long time. Even Amanda. How much of their new attitude had to do with Maria?

His mind was so tangled up in thoughts of his beautiful neighbor that he wasn't sure he could even think straight anymore.

Before they reached the house, they saw Jillian coming toward them as she pushed Sammy in a stroller. Kelsey immediately ran to greet her. Smiling, Jillian relinquished the stroller to Kelsey and glanced back at Grady, who was still lagging behind. "Sam called from the barn and said he'd be back at the house as soon as all the horses are taken care of. So you'll have some adult male company in a few minutes."

Grady chuckled. "That's okay. I'm used to being outnumbered by women. At home and on the job."

"Speaking of jobs—" Jillian looked over at Maria "—Grady and I are registered to attend the annual conference for nonprofit organizations dedicated to services for older people. It starts on Monday."

"I've heard that conference is very good," Maria said.

"Me, too, but I got a call this afternoon from the director of one of my mission groups. He's coming into town unexpectedly, and I really do need to meet with him. That means I can't go to the conference."

"So I'll be going by myself?" Grady asked as they reached the deck at the back of the house.

Jillian lifted Sammy from the stroller and climbed the steps to the deck. "No, I've already paid the fees, so I want Maria to go in my place." She glanced at Maria. "That won't be a problem, will it?"

Grady noticed Maria's hesitant smile as she looked from Jillian to him and back at Jillian. "I don't believe I have anything pressing on my schedule for the beginning of next week. When were you planning to leave?"

"We have a flight to Seattle tomorrow evening. I'll change my ticket so it'll be in your name and I'll call the hotel and change the room registration." Jillian set Sammy on the deck.

Kelsey immediately began to play with the little boy. He giggled and ran away, and she chased him around the deck.

"What time's the flight?" Maria asked, still looking less than excited about the trip.

"Around seven-thirty," he replied, hoping her uncertainty didn't have anything to do with having to spend time with him. "We can ride out to the airport together."

Maria gave him another tentative smile. "That should work."

Jillian gave Maria a quick hug. "I really appreciate your rearranging your schedule for me."

"You're the boss."

"I never think of myself as the boss." Jillian laughed.

"Oh, you're the boss, all right." Sam joined her on the deck and gave her a peck on the cheek. "But if you have to have a boss, I can't think of a better one to have."

"Somehow I think he just makes me think I'm the boss." Jillian playfully swatted at Sam then turned her attention to Maria. "Let me get the brochures and stuff that I have for the conference."

As Jillian disappeared into the house, Grady watched Maria, trying to gauge her reaction. He wished he could read her thoughts. Or maybe that wouldn't be wise. He might find out she wasn't looking forward to their forced togetherness. Oh, well, this was his chance to spend time alone with her. Without kids. Without family. Without interfering friends. What would he discover? Was he ready to find out?

Chapter Thirteen

Maria settled in the front seat of Grady's car. Amanda, with her iPod, and Kelsey, with a book Jillian had given her, jumped into the back. Grady still stood next to the car, talking with Sam and Jillian. As the girls jostled for position and buckled their seat belts, Maria tried to brush away the thought that kept nudging at the corners of her mind. This seemed like a family—Grady, the girls and her. She tried shoving the idea away, but it had taken up permanent residence in her brain.

The upcoming trip with Grady would make the thought even more difficult to eradicate. Time alone with him was all this seed of an idea needed to establish deep roots in the garden of her mind. Throw in the laughter of two girls for fertilizer and the thought would take over like weeds in fertile ground.

She had to remember that she would be moving to her new house soon. That would take her away from any temptation to get drawn further into their family circle. Maybe a stop at her new house would cement that thinking.

Grady opened the door and slipped behind the wheel

as he said goodbye to Sam and Jillian. Trying not to look at Grady, Maria waved as they drove away. Then she stared out the window at the passing scenery without really seeing it.

When they reached the main road, Kelsey tapped Maria on the shoulder. "I forgot to say thanks for coming and letting me ride with you. I had the best time ever."

"Me, too." The feelings she had been trying to push away all afternoon shimmered around her heart like the sun that sat just above the tops of the evergreens lining the road. It was no use. Her mind overflowed with emotion. She swallowed the lump that rose in her throat. "You're welcome, Kelsey."

"Dad, can we eat out tonight and invite Maria?" Kelsey asked.

"Maybe Maria has other plans." Grady glanced her way then turned his attention back to the road.

Maria couldn't tell what he was thinking from that hurried look. But she feared seeing an expression of irritation at having her pushed on him again. He couldn't very well say no, with her sitting right there. She couldn't forget how, just this morning, Amanda and Kelsey—especially Kelsey—had maneuvered Grady into taking her on the trail ride when he seemed reluctant to do it. Now they were doing it again.

"Do you have other plans?" Kelsey leaned forward in her seat as she strained against the seat belt.

Maria turned toward the backseat. "Well, actually, I was going to drive out and see how things are progressing at my new house."

"See." Grady said without hesitation. "She's busy."

"We could take her to see her new house. Can we do that? Please, Dad?"

The interior of the car grew silent. Grady didn't answer immediately. He appeared to be thinking over his daughter's suggestion. The drone of the engine and the hum of the tires against the road seemed loud in the quiet.

Then he chuckled, breaking the silence. "Maybe she's seen enough of us for one day."

"Have you?" Kelsey asked.

A knot formed in Maria's chest at the dejected tone in Kelsey's voice. "No, I'd love to have you see my house."

"Yippee!"

Maria didn't have to turn around to know that Kelsey was bouncing in her seat. And out of the corner of her eye, she saw Amanda, who had seemed to be lost in her iPod, extend her hand across the seat and without missing a beat give her sister five. The two girls had their matchmaking routine down to a science. Had Grady noticed his children's conspiracy?

A smile nipped at the corners of his mouth. "So how do we get there?"

Letting his response lift her spirits, Maria gave him directions. In a few minutes he turned onto the road that led to her new home. Several other houses under construction lined the blacktop road that wound its way through forestland.

"Which one's yours?" Kelsey asked.

"Mine's at the end of the road. The one with the beige siding and brick trim." A flutter of anticipation filled her chest as she viewed her soon-to-be home.

Grady pulled into the driveway behind several pickup trucks. "Looks like someone's here working, even on the weekend."

"That means the house should be finished on time." Maria exited the car.

Grady looked at her as they walked to the front door. "And when will that be?"

"As soon as they do the last of the trim work and lay the carpet."

"That soon, huh?"

"Yeah. I'm excited."

"I'm sure you are."

Wondering about Grady's response to her timeline, Maria opened the door while Kelsey and Amanda stood nearby. He almost seemed disappointed that she would be moving so soon. She gave herself a mental shake. *Don't read anything into it.*

Grady lagged behind as they entered the house. Pounding hammers and the buzz of a saw greeted them. The smell of fresh paint wafted through the air.

"Wow! I like this!" Kelsey stopped short in the foyer and glanced around. "Where's all the noise coming from?"

"The basement. They're finishing a rec room for me down there."

"You're going to live here all by yourself?" Kelsey asked, her eyes wide with curiosity. "Won't you get lonely?"

"Hopefully I'll have lots of visitors." Maria winked at Kelsey.

Kelsey looked over at Grady, who stood silhouetted in the doorway. "We can visit her, can't we?"

Grady nodded as he stepped into the house. For an instant, Maria imagined him coming *home* to this house, not just coming for a visit. Her breath caught in her throat and she immediately erased the thought. She couldn't go there. Not now. She was in a vulnerable frame of mind and couldn't deal with all the thoughts that bombarded her. What was it about this day that had put all kinds of crazy ideas in her head?

"What's that room?" Kelsey pointed to the room on her right, taking Maria's attention away from Grady.

Maria walked to the center of the room and stood under the chandelier hanging from the tray ceiling. "What's your guess?"

"My guess is it's a dining room," Amanda replied, still listening to her music.

"Right," Maria said.

"I want to guess the next room." Kelsey raced around the corner. "I know this one. It's the kitchen."

Her voice bounced around the empty rooms as Maria and Grady joined her.

In a moment, Amanda came around the corner. She stopped and looked at Kelsey. "Oh, how lame. It was *really* hard to figure out this was the kitchen with the sink and all the cabinets and stuff in here."

Kelsey pranced around the breakfast bar and twirled around on the plywood subflooring. "This is the living room. And I think I can guess all the rest without your help." She took off through the rest of the house, calling out the bedrooms and baths as she went.

Maria laughed and looked at Amanda. "Do you suppose your sister even realizes we haven't gone with her?"

Shrugging, Amanda quirked an eyebrow. "Sometimes I don't even claim her." Then she moseyed over to the French doors overlooking the deck. She opened them and went outside.

Kelsey returned. "I named them all. Did you hear?"

"Yes," Grady replied. "Now it's time to calm down."

"I love this house." Ignoring her cast, she clapped her

hands together. "Daddy, can we get a house like this one? You said we'd get a new house when we moved here. Why haven't we got one yet?"

Grady laughed. "Did you finally run out of breath?"

Kelsey stood with her arms akimbo and glared at her father. "I'm tired of sharing a room with Amanda."

Amanda returned from the deck and stood in the doorway. "And I'm tired of sharing a room with *her*."

Shaking his head, Grady blew out a long breath. "I know. I know. Maybe we'll have to build a house, too, because I didn't like anything the Realtor showed me. And I just haven't taken the time to look again."

"Maybe we can build a house next to Maria's." Kelsey's face brightened.

"Kelsey, that's a terrible idea. Do you want to live out here in the boonies?" Amanda motioned for Kelsey to come with her as she stepped back onto the deck. "Look. We're in the country. Who would you play with?"

Maria's stomach sank. Her silly mind had let her imagination go wild with ideas about having a family. Grady's family. But Amanda's statement had brought her back to reality. Grady had never indicated he had an interest in her. Or had he? She remembered last night and the way he had looked at her as if he had wanted to kiss her. She hadn't imagined that. But how had she jumped from a possible kiss to thinking about marriage, especially to a man like Grady?

He didn't love her. He was a workaholic. And most important of all, he didn't share her faith. These things ought to make her realize she had ignored the truth of the situation.

"I don't care. I like it here." Kelsey ran and threw her arms around Maria. "And I love Maria."

"And I love you, too, sweetheart." Blinking back the tears welling up in her eyes, Maria held Kelsey tight. How she would love to hear those words from Grady. The thought froze her. She was falling in love with a man who was all wrong for her. Wrong for everything she wanted.

Amanda and Kelsey scrambled out of the car and grabbed some of their belongings from the trunk. Beth stepped onto the front porch as the girls, with suitcases in hand hurried up the walk. Carrying the remaining pieces of luggage, Grady followed, amazed that even Amanda seemed excited about spending several days with Beth and Max while Clay was out of town. He speculated that her enthusiasm came from the hope of seeing some of Max's friends up close and personal.

Kelsey waved as she adjusted her backpack on her shoulders. "Hi, Aunt Beth."

"Hi, girls." Beth held open the door. "Max will show you where you're going to be staying."

Max appeared and took the suitcases from Amanda and Kelsey. As Grady watched them go, he suddenly worried that they wouldn't get along and would cause Beth problems, especially since Clay wasn't there. What if Amanda sulked and pouted the whole time and Kelsey talked nonstop and aggravated her sister?

Anxiety knotted Grady's stomach. He used to leave them with his mother or his mother-in-law without a second thought. He had done that all too often. The girls' less-than-stellar behavior at times probably stemmed from his inattention over the past few years. He tried not to worry. He was probably tying himself in knots for nothing.

Or maybe his anxiety came from the thought of having to spend three whole days with Maria. Three days without the buffer of children, family or friends. There would probably be a lot of one-on-one conversation. And he wasn't sure he was ready to deal with that. With the way he was thinking lately, he wasn't sure his romantic feelings for Maria wouldn't spill over into their business relationship. Would that be wise?

"Do we need to bring in anything else?" Beth asked.

Startled out of his thoughts, Grady nodded. "You're going to think they're moving in, with all the stuff they've brought."

"Well, girls need lots of stuff." Beth accompanied Grady to the car for the rest of their things. "I'm glad Amanda and Kelsey are going to participate in the program the youth are putting on at church."

"Yeah, I guess they'll have fun." Grady handed her pillows he picked up from the backseat.

"You don't sound too sure."

Grady took in Beth's comment and considered her possible motives in bringing up the subject. He kept remembering how Clay had told him he should talk to Beth about her experiences. Would talking with her help—or just cause more confusion?

Grady shrugged. "If that works for them, then it's fine."

"That's the way I felt when Max started getting involved with the youth group."

"Are you bringing up this church business for a reason?" Grady asked.

"I'm glad you let the girls go to church with us, and I thought maybe you'd like to talk about it sometime."

"I suppose Clay put you up to this," Grady said.

A little smile curved Beth's lips. "No, this conversation was my idea."

"So what are you trying to tell me?"

"I guess maybe that it's okay to doubt sometimes, but don't let it simmer."

"I think it's too late for that. The doubt's been simmering ever since Nina died." Grady glanced away. Even after all this time, he still felt the hurt when he talked about his dead wife. "I just saw too much hypocrisy in the church. People saying one thing but doing another."

"I know what you mean about the hypocrisy."

"How's that?"

"My dad was a preacher."

"He was?"

"Yeah. I'm a PK. Preacher's kid. Clay never told you?"

"No," Grady replied with a halfhearted laugh. "I pretty much shut him out when he started talking about church. So what about the hypocrisy?"

"I saw it all. Church folks fighting, gossiping and doing all the stuff they weren't supposed to do." Beth sighed. "I think the thing that bothered me most was how badly they treated my mom sometimes, when she tried so hard to please. Then I rebelled, and my parents didn't handle that well. So I wound up in trouble and estranged from my parents, God and the church."

"What brought you back?"

Beth smiled. "Your brother and some folks from church here. Sam's sister, Kim, had befriended me before Clay came, but he made it awfully hard to ignore God."

"Was he always preaching to you?"

"Not really. Is he doing that to you?" Concern knit her brow.

"Only once—when he told me I should talk to you— but once was enough." Grady gazed at his normally shy sister-in-law and realized what it must have taken for her to step forward and talk to him. Maybe he ought to listen. "So what are you trying to tell me?"

"Just what I learned. You can't always rely on people. They make mistakes. But you can rely on God."

Grady glanced away. Was that what he'd been doing? Looking at people instead of God? But why had God allowed all this bad stuff to happen in the first place? He didn't have an answer and he couldn't possibly tell Beth about Nina's affair. He looked back at her. "That isn't always clear to me."

"Well, just give church here a try."

Beth tapped her fingers against her leg and stared at him without breathing, as if she were waiting for some kind of explosion. Smiling, he stepped closer and gave her shoulders a squeeze. "Just for you. I'll do it just for you."

"Not just for me. For you. And Amanda and Kelsey, too. It's nice to be together as a family," she replied, not quite meeting his gaze as a pleased little smile curved her mouth.

Family. The word rang through his mind. Maria. Her name wound its way into that family-thinking thing. He was going to have to deal with these feelings sooner or later. The next few days with Maria, starting with their trip to the airport, might be a good time. Did he dare act on his feelings for Maria?

Three days later Grady walked through the parking garage at the airport in Spokane. He punched his keyless remote and heard the click that let him know the door was unlocked. That click also signaled the beginning of real time alone with Maria—something he had managed to avoid during the entire conference by spending the days and evenings with other attendees. On the flights there and back, they hadn't sat together because he had been asked to move to help distribute the weight in the small commuter plane.

In the beginning he had welcomed the reprieve from having to face time alone with Maria. But as the conference continued, he'd had the paranoid feeling that she might be trying to avoid him, rather than the other way around. Even the trips to and from the airports had been filled with conference talk, except for a brief conversation about how Amanda and Kelsey were doing.

When he popped the trunk, Maria handed him her bag. Smiling, she continued to talk almost nonstop about the conference, much as she had done since they had gotten off the plane and walked through the airport to the parking garage. She seemed oblivious to his discomfort. Or maybe she recognized it and was just trying to fill the silence with chatter.

Chicken.

That word described his behavior for the past three days. He'd been afraid to face how he cared about Maria, how his daughters loved her and how she felt about him. And, yet, despite his fear, it was becoming evident that he was falling in love with her.

But the idea of loving again twisted his insides into knots of worry that he'd make the same mistakes again or let down the people he cared about. That was selfish thinking. When he let anxiety rule, he *was* thinking of himself—of the hurt he might suffer—not of the feelings of the ones he loved.

It was time to quit being a coward.

Glancing at his watch, he slid behind the steering wheel. A little past five o'clock. He looked over at Maria, who was buckling her seat belt. His pulse racing, he took a deep breath. "Would you like to have dinner in Spokane before we head back to Pinecrest?"

Her face lit up with a smile. "Yes, I'd like that. Do you know a good restaurant?"

"Yeah, Jillian and Sam told me about their favorite pizza place, if you don't mind pizza."

"Pizza's good, especially after eating conference banquet food for three days."

Grady chuckled. "Yeah, you can eat just so much of that. Besides, I haven't had my weekly pizza fix. That's a staple with the girls and me."

"And hot dogs, as I recall."

"That's Kelsey's favorite. Can't understand that one."

"I can. There's nothing better than a big, juicy hot dog, slightly charred, plastered with mustard in a soft, fat bun."

Maria's description of her ideal hot dog made Grady laugh out loud. "And you kidded me about burning marshmallows?"

"Oh, but there's a difference between burnt and slightly charred."

"Would you like to demonstrate that sometime?"

"Are you asking me to treat you to my gourmet hot-dog meal?"

"If that's what it takes."

"Okay, after I get moved into my new house, I'll have you and the girls over for hot dogs."

"Amanda and Kelsey will be glad to hear that. I talked to them right after we got off the plane. They're headed to church for supper and then practice for the youth program."

"And how do you feel about that?"

Grady wondered why she was asking. Would his participation in church raise his standing in her mind? "I've decided if that's what they want, I'm all for it. Beth even convinced me to give it a try."

Grady didn't miss the surprise on Maria's face as she turned to him. "I'm glad."

"I thought you'd say that." As he looked at her, he realized how much he wanted her approval. But was he doing what he had faulted others for doing—going to church with ulterior motives? He pushed the question aside.

A little later, when they entered the restaurant, the smell of freshly baked pizza greeted them. Laughter and lively conversation filled the air. While they waited for their pizza, Maria continued to talk about the things she had learned at the conference. Her enthusiasm reminded him of Kelsey. Maria's zest for life was just one more thing that sparked his interest.

"I can hardly wait to tell Jillian about the organization that funds dreams for senior citizens. I know she'll be interested in having the foundation do something similar." Gazing at him, Maria took a sip of her drink. "I was so inspired by what they've done to enrich older people's lives."

"We can always start doing that on a small scale at the facility in Pinecrest."

Maria nodded. "Let's talk about it next week."

"Sure. Let me know when," Grady said as they got their pizza.

While they ate, he wondered whether he'd ever get up enough courage to discuss anything besides business with Maria. Did she always look at him in the context of work, as a guy who spent too much time at the office? He deserved that label, even though he was trying to change. Maybe now that the facility was open, things would settle down and he could make that change. But wasn't that his usual procedure—seeing tomorrow as always more convenient?

"What was the highlight of the conference for you?" She took a big bite of her pizza while she waited for his answer.

Being with you. The words were on the tip of his tongue, but fear of her reaction—a possible rejection—kept him from saying them aloud. He should let her know how much her presence meant to him, but he couldn't just blurt it out of the blue. Somehow, the right time would come.

Maria talked constantly between bites of pizza. It was almost as if she was afraid to let the conversation lag. Maybe she was feeling as awkward as he did. But was it for the same reason?

Grady downed the last of his drink, then set the glass on the table. "Finished?"

Maria nodded. "Guess we should head home."

Grady didn't want the evening to end. This was where he had to take the step he had been avoiding for three days. "Have you ever visited Riverfront Park?"

"No, but I've wanted to." She folded her napkin and placed it on the table.

"How about now? It's only a block or so from here and we still have about an hour of daylight." Grady held his breath as he waited for her answer.

"Sure. I'm wearing my walking shoes."

Grady smiled with relief and got up from the table. "I promised Amanda and Kelsey we'd come some Saturday and go to the IMAX Theater," he said, thinking how much he wanted Maria to come when he brought the girls. He could ask her, but putting it off till later seemed like the smart thing to do—or maybe it was the cowardly thing to do.

"They'll enjoy a day at the park."

"I hope so," he replied, telling himself again that he would ask her later. "I never know with Amanda, but things are getting better with her. Thanks to you."

Maria gave him a sidelong glance as they left the restaurant. "How's that?"

"Your suggestion about the iPod worked. She jumped at the chance to help me download songs."

"That's because she wants your attention, even if she doesn't act like it."

"I'm beginning to see that." Grady had realized a lot of things lately—like how Maria brightened his day with her presence. Was he brave enough to tell her?

While they walked, he had the urge to hold her hand, but he didn't. He just wasn't sure of how to go about this. Because of his quiet, serious nature, he'd never done much dating. He'd only had a few dates in high school and his first couple years of college. During his junior year he'd met Nina, a freshman, and he'd fallen for her immediately. They married the summer between his college graduation and law school. It had been years since he'd dated or even thought about it. Would he make a mess of things if he got involved with another woman?

Then there was the matter of his kids. How did they fit into this scenario? Maria seemed to love them, but he remembered her statement concerning Clay and how he had decided to adopt Max. *I'm not sure how I would feel about taking on the lifelong responsibility of someone else's child.*

The words burned a hole in his soul. Was that what held him back? Maybe he just needed to take this one step at a time, not rush ahead in his thinking. He only wanted to ask for a date, not make a marriage proposal.

All these thoughts bombarded him as they entered the park.

"What are all those lights?" he asked, gazing at the towering network of cables that twinkled in the twilight.

"It's the U.S. Pavilion from Expo '74. The IMAX Theater is right next to it."

"I thought you said you've never been here."

"I haven't, but I've seen brochures." Maria pointed to her right. "There's the carousel."

"Would you like to take a ride?"

She grinned. "That might ruin your stuffy image."

"You're calling me stuffy? You wound me." He put his hand on his chest, but he laughed.

"I didn't call *you* stuffy. Just your image."

"Let's ruin it." Without taking the time to think about the consequences, Grady grabbed Maria's hand and pulled her toward the carousel.

After purchasing tickets, they rode side by side on two of the beautiful hand-carved horses, while merry organ music played over the sound system. Grady hadn't felt so lighthearted in years. Just being with Maria made everything brighter.

When the ride ended, he dismounted and looked at Maria, whose horse had stopped in a high position. "Need some help getting down?"

"Yeah." Her eyes reflected the lights from the carousel.

He gazed up at her. "Put your hands on my shoulders."

She swiveled around on the horse until she sat side-saddle facing him. Putting one foot in the stirrup, she did as he instructed. While she slid down, he balanced her in his hands. Their gazes held, and he forgot to breathe as he set her down. They stood so close he could have kissed her, but then he stepped away, still fearful of his feelings.

"Thanks." She looked away, almost as if she felt as awkward as he did.

If only he could read her mind and know how she viewed him, he might be brave enough to let her know how he felt. Trying to focus his mind on something else, he said, "Kelsey will love this, but I'm not sure about Amanda. She might think it's for kids."

Maria followed him out of the building where the carousel was housed. "Then you should take her on the Skyride. It's right over there."

"Great. Let's give it a try."

She slipped her hand into his again as they made their way to the ride. His heart soared like the gondola cars that took them over the Spokane River and the falls.

"Is this a trial run of the park and I'm the guinea pig?" she asked when they emerged from the gondola car.

This was the right time to let her know his feelings. He swallowed hard. "No, tonight is just about you and me."

She stared at him in the waning light. "What about us?"

"Maria, I know I treated you badly in the past. I hope you've forgiven me."

"You shouldn't have to ask me again." She blinked, and the surrounding lights sparkled in her eyes. "You know I have."

"I just wanted to be sure, because I think I'm falling in love with you." He pulled her into his arms, and he breathed easier when she put her arms around his waist and laid her head on his chest. "Can you take a chance on me?"

Chapter Fourteen

Maria wanted to say yes, but something held her back. The disappointments and hurt of her childhood continued to color her thoughts concerning Grady. The present and the past warred in her mind as she stood in his embrace—a place that felt so right.

So many things about him reached out to her, but was she ready to deal with her feelings if he turned out to be the same workaholic she'd always known? He'd shown that he was trying to change. He was even going to start attending church again. That counted for a lot. *Take a chance and see where it leads.* The phrase played through her thoughts.

She stepped out of his embrace and looked up at him. "Are you asking me for a date?"

A smile brightened his eyes, but he stared at her as if he wasn't quite sure of her response. "So if I ask you to go with me to Kelsey's fall festival, you'll say yes?"

His uncertainty touched something deep inside her. "Yes."

Laughing, he pulled her close again. "That's a relief. I haven't asked someone out in a long time."

"And you thought I might say no?"

"I considered that possibility." Grady held her at arm's length, a grin adding to his handsome features. "After all, I wasn't exactly on your favorites list when I moved here."

"I wasn't on yours, either." She gave him an impish look. "So you think you're on my favorites list now?"

"If not, I'm trying hard to get there, because you're definitely on mine." He put an arm around her shoulders and drew her close.

She couldn't help grinning. "Okay, I'll admit you're on mine, and you've even moved up a few notches."

"Only a few?"

"Well, maybe more than a few, but I didn't want to give you a big head by telling you how many."

"Or telling me how low I ranked to begin with, but thanks for keeping me humble." He chuckled. "And thanks for making me laugh. I haven't done much of that in the past few years."

"You're welcome."

They laughed together again, but Grady's statement reminded her that he was getting over a lot of hurt. She wanted to help him heal his emotional scars, so she wasn't going to rush into anything. But when she gazed up at him, her pulse raced. She cared about this man. Still, the thought of a relationship with him scared her. It brought expectations that meant putting aside all the things she'd thought she wanted. But she was determined to figure out what she really yearned to do with her life.

Just enjoying each other's company, they walked hand in hand back to the car. The fading light cast a golden glow in the sky and on the nearby buildings, as if to signal something golden about the decision they had made.

While they rode back to Pinecrest, they talked a little more about the conference. Then their conversation drifted to their plans for the festival. Maria gazed at Grady in the car's darkened interior. This was really happening. She and Grady were going on a date.

"What do you think will happen when you tell Amanda and Kelsey about our date?" Maria asked, wondering whether Grady had considered their feelings.

"Kelsey'll probably give you one of her bear hugs. So watch out for that cast." Grady laughed. "I don't know how Amanda will react, but she *won't* be unhappy. They haven't been exactly subtle in their attempts to get us together."

"You think?" Maria joined in his laughter as he pulled the car into the garage. "It looks like your matchmakers are home."

Chuckling, Grady got the suitcases out of the trunk. "You'd better get your armor ready to ward off that cast, but not before I do this." He grabbed her hand and pulled her into his arms. She gazed up at him. The yard light illuminated his face. "I've wanted to do this ever since I watched you eating toasted marshmallows at the campout."

Maria put her arms around his neck and pulled him closer. She closed her eyes and drank in the touch of his lips on hers. Her heart felt as though it was home. She was lost in his embrace until she heard applause and laughter.

Her insides jittery, she sprang away from Grady.

Kelsey ran into the yard. "Daddy, we saw you kissing Maria."

When Kelsey reached Grady, he scooped her up into his arms. "Is that all right with you?"

"Yeah."

"And me, too." Amanda gave Kelsey a high five when Grady set her back on the ground.

Then Beth and Max joined them, and everyone started talking at once as they made their way toward the house. Once they were inside, more laughter accented the hugs and handshakes. Despite the joy radiating through Maria's mind, she realized how many hopes were built around her and Grady's developing relationship. Some of her earlier fear niggled at the back of her mind.

God, please help me do this right. The silent prayer lingered in her thoughts as they said good-night to Beth and Max.

While Amanda and Kelsey unpacked their suitcases, Kelsey elected herself the date planner for the festival. The child brimmed with so much excitement that she couldn't hold still. After Grady got her calmed down enough to get her into bed, he read her a story. Even Amanda, who usually didn't show much emotion, didn't try to hide her excitement about the upcoming weekend.

Finally, when everything was as normal as possible, Grady walked Maria up to her apartment. They stopped just inside the door, and Grady took her into his arms. "Thanks for putting up with all that craziness. This has been one of the best days of my life."

Maria smiled up at him. "Mine, too, and I loved being a part of it, craziness and all."

"Even all the behind-the-scenes matchmaking?"

"Even that." Nodding, Maria smiled wider. "I had to laugh when Beth said Jillian was telling everyone this trip would finally bring us together."

"Guess she was right." He leaned closer and gave her a quick kiss. "I'll see you tomorrow night for pizza, as soon as Kelsey and I get home. Then Friday's the football game and Saturday the festival."

"It's a good thing Kelsey appointed herself your social secretary."

"A very good thing." Smiling, Grady blew her a kiss as he left.

Maria sighed with contentment as she closed the door and leaned against it. What a day! Her whole life had taken a complete turn. She had never dreamed that this man, who had spent more time with his laptop and the other conferees during their trip than with her, would suddenly announce that he was falling in love with her. Closing her eyes, she wrapped her arms around herself, as if doing so would preserve the happiness that bubbled inside her. She prayed that it would last.

On a Saturday morning two weeks after the fall festival, Maria watched as a moving van filled with the furniture she'd had in storage in California parked in front of her new house. Since the closing earlier in the week, she had little by little moved most of her things from the apartment to her new home. Boxes full of her possessions lay scattered throughout the rooms. Today she would pack up the rest and make the final move.

Just as she finished talking to the driver, Grady pulled his car into her driveway. Maria's breath hitched when he got out and waved. No matter how much time they shared, it was still a thrill to see him, especially the lopsided grin that appeared whenever he looked her way. She went to sleep each night with his image imprinted on her mind.

After jumping out of the backseat, Kelsey raced across the yard and greeted her with a big hug. Amanda, sporting her iPod, as usual, sauntered over with her father.

"Looks like the movers are right on time." Grady gave Maria a peck on the cheek. "Hey, I've got to stop by the center this morning, but I thought I'd drop the girls off before I went. I'll be back in about an hour. Okay?" He gave her shoulders a squeeze as he kissed her cheek again.

"Sure, I'll be waiting for you."

"Bye." He waved as he sprinted to his car.

Maria tried to smile, but a sick little knot developed in her stomach as she watched him drive away. Would he be back in an hour? She shouldn't question his statement, but she had seen the old pattern emerging over the past week. He had called her a couple of times to pick up Kelsey from the after-school program because he was running late. He had always come home in time to join them for the supper they had planned, but she wondered whether she was allowing him to lapse into his former ways. No, it wasn't that bad. Maybe if she kept telling herself that, she might even believe it.

"What do you want us to do?" Kelsey grabbed Maria's arm and dragged her toward the house.

"Let's see. I think I'll have you put away books to begin with," Maria replied, deciding not to worry over nothing. Grady would be back when he said. After all, the past two weeks had been filled with laughter and more happiness than she had ever hoped to have.

While she got Amanda and Kelsey started with their jobs and showed the movers where to put her belongings, she tried to brush away her worries. She set her mind to recalling how funny Grady had been while he was in the dunking tank and how much fun it had been to send him splashing into the water. She thought about the quiet evenings they had spent snuggled together on his couch while they watched a movie. Her pulse zinged when she relived the kisses they had shared and remembered how sometimes it had been hard to say goodnight. And most important of all, she thought of how wonderful it felt to sit in church with Grady and his girls. Everything seemed so perfect, but had she ignored the subtle signs that all wasn't completely wonderful?

Now that she had moved, what would happen? Was everything already falling apart? No, she wouldn't think the worst. Grady loved her. Her gaze traveled to the kitchen counter and the bouquet of red roses that he had sent her. She picked up the card and read it again. *Congratulations! I love you, Grady.*

Checking off the items the movers brought into the house, Maria tried not to look at the clock. But when they took a break for lunch, she couldn't ignore the time anymore. Her stomach rumbled. Even though she didn't feel like eating, she called the girls into the kitchen, where they made sandwiches and munched on chips and apple slices. While she forced down the food, negative thoughts plagued her. It was all starting to unravel, but she kept making excuses in her mind, because she didn't want to believe it was happening.

"Where's my dad?" Kelsey looked at Maria.

"Oh, he got stuck at the office again. That always happens to him." Amanda tapped her little sister on the head. "You ought to know that by now, Kels."

Maria tried to put a happy face on the situation. "I'm sure he'll be along when he finishes his work."

Taking the last bite of her sandwich, Kelsey hopped

down from the barstool and stood with her arms akimbo. "Well, I'm going to tell him he should've been here."

If the circumstances hadn't been so sad, Maria would've laughed at Kelsey's pronouncement. What was Grady doing that had made him forget his daughters and the woman he supposedly loved? His job. Maybe that would always be his first love.

Hoping not to display any negative feelings, Maria gave the girls another chore. The movers returned from lunch, and Maria had something to take her mind off Grady. During the afternoon, she made great progress toward putting her house in order. Jillian and Beth stopped by for a while to lend a hand. Maria was thankful they didn't ask about Grady.

Finally, the movers brought in the last piece of furniture and put together the last bed. Grady wasn't here. He had promised he'd return, but like so many other promises he'd made, he hadn't kept it. He hadn't even called. Although she wanted to cry, she didn't dare let Amanda and Kelsey see that she was upset. But she couldn't deny that all her dreams were crashing down around her.

"Looks like you're all moved in." Her pulse pounded all over her body as she turned to see Grady step into the room.

"What kept you?" she asked, trying to remain calm.

"I'm so sorry I didn't make it back. Let me take you out to dinner to make up for it."

Afraid she would cry if she continued to look at him, she turned away. "I don't think that would be a good idea. I still have a lot to do."

"I can help you later."

"No, it's too late."

He touched her arm. "Maria."

Jerking away, she turned to face him, anger overcoming her tears. "Didn't you hear me? It's too late. You're too late."

"Daddy!" Kelsey bounded into the room. "You got here!" She twirled around with her arms in the air. "Doesn't Maria's house look fabo with all the furniture in it?"

"Yeah, it does. Where's your sister?"

"She's putting towels in the linen closet."

"You can help her finish. Then we'll get something to eat."

As Kelsey left, Maria escaped outside. The late-afternoon sun still warmed the deck, but it couldn't warm the cold swirling through her troubled mind.

Grady followed. "You're angry with me?"

With a huge ache filling her chest, Maria ignored his question and just stared at him. "What was your first clue? What was so important that you had to work on a Saturday?" She didn't wait for an answer as the words tumbled out. She gritted her teeth in order to keep from yelling. "Or so urgent that you couldn't even call?"

"Some people wanted a tour—"

"I'm sorry," she said, interrupting him. "I really don't want to hear your explanation." She pinched the bridge of her nose. How many times would work come before anything else in his life? He was just like her father—a confirmed workaholic. She didn't want that kind of life. "You said you were trying to change, but I can't wait around and hope it happens. Just leave."

"I make one little slip and you want to throw it all away?"

"It's not one little slip, Grady. It's a pattern. One you can't seem to break." Closing her eyes, she took a deep breath. When she finally looked at him, she couldn't miss the misery in his eyes. But she wouldn't let that sway her. "Believe me. It's better this way. Our contact will be limited now that I've moved. Please make it easy on both of us. Make your excuses to the girls and go."

"What am I going to tell them?"

"I don't know. That's something you'll have to figure out."

"I love you."

"That's what you say, but your actions say something else. You love your job more than anything."

"That's not true." He narrowed his gaze. "Can't you forgive me?"

"This isn't about forgiveness. It's about making the best decision for you, for me, *and* for Amanda and Kelsey." Maria glanced up. Her chest filled with pain when she saw Kelsey standing just inside the door. What had she heard?

When Kelsey turned and ran out of the house, Maria knew the child had heard too much.

Carrying a bag of trash, Grady walked across the backyard. The bright sunshine glinting off the garbage can in the alley next to the garage contradicted the forecast of rain. He shivered in the cool morning air as he dumped the bag into the can. The lid clanged as he put it back.

Heading to the house, he glanced at the steps leading to the empty upstairs apartment. He speculated about what Maria was doing today. Nothing had been right since the day she moved. Even though he saw her when he took the girls to church, his attendance hadn't changed her opinion of him. She probably guessed he was going to church for the wrong reasons and, that deep down inside, he still harbored doubts about God—doubts that he hadn't taken the time to deal with.

Besides, she was still disappointed over his failure to return on the day of her move. She refused to talk to him. All business communication came through her assistant or Jillian. When he walked back into the house, the sound of a vacuum filled the air. Kelsey and Amanda were busy doing their Saturday chores. The ringing of the phone sounded over the whine of the vacuum. He strode across the kitchen to answer it.

After answering, he listened with a sinking heart as the head nurse on duty told him that one of the Alzheimer's patients had wandered off, despite all the security measures at the assisted-living center.

"Do you want me to call the police?"

Her question shot through his brain. The police. The gravity of the situation hit Grady hard. "Before we do that, be sure he's not somewhere in the building."

"We've done that. We've checked everywhere. In the building and outside. He's gone. One of the CNAs and our maintenance guy are already looking in the surrounding neighborhood." Panic sounded in her voice.

"Then, you'd better call the police." Grady rubbed a hand across his forehead to suppress his anger. The last thing he needed to do was yell at one of his trusted nurses. She needed reassuring words, not criticism. "He probably hasn't gone far."

"I hope you're right. I don't understand how he got out. All the security systems are working."

"We'll find him. I'll be there in a few minutes." Hanging up the phone, he wondered how this could have happened.

He stood in the middle of the kitchen and stared at the ceiling. *Why, God? Why is all this stuff happening to me?* He had promised the girls they would go into Spokane today after they finished their work. He didn't know how he was going to tell them he had to go to work, especially after what had happened with Maria.

Sighing, he dragged himself into the living room, where Kelsey was dusting and Amanda was pushing the vacuum around the room as if she was trying for a speed-vacuuming record. When she saw him, she stopped.

"Hey, girls, I've got some bad news."

Amanda shut off the vacuum. "What?"

"It's about our plans for today. Something's come up at work and I have to go to the center for a little while."

Frowning, Amanda stamped one sneaker-clad foot on the floor. "Oh, you are always doing this. Every time we have plans, something comes up at your dumb job."

Grady took a deep breath. "You have a right to be angry, but this can't be helped." He explained and hoped they'd understand. "After we find our patient, there'll probably still be time to go into Spokane. So while I'm gone, finish your work, so you'll be ready when I get back. Okay?"

"Okay." Amanda's familiar pout resurrected itself as she turned on the vacuum. Her dismissal was clear.

Kelsey didn't say anything. She just started dusting again. But Grady didn't miss her hangdog look. She had never said anything about Maria, but her silence hurt more than any accusation could have.

"I'll call you when I know something." He hurried out the back door and tried not to think about how he was disappointing his children.

When he arrived at the center, Nancy, the head nurse, rushed out to greet him. "I'm so glad you're here. We still don't have a clue where Mr. Corbin is."

"Show me his room." Grady followed her into the Alzheimer's wing of the building. "You've checked with the staff to be sure all the doors were secure, right?"

"Yes, he ate breakfast and then returned to his room." She motioned toward the eating area as they passed by.

"So as far as you know, he was in his room until he disappeared?"

"Yes." She opened the door.

"How did you discover he was gone?" Grady glanced around the room for clues that might help them figure out how the man had escaped from what was considered a secure unit.

"His daughter-in-law called. When he didn't answer his phone, she called the main phone line."

Grady rubbed his temples in an effort to ward off the headache that began to build. "So his family knows he's gone?"

"Yes. They're on their way here." Nancy patted him on the arm. "I'm glad you're here to deal with them."

"Did they seem upset?" Grady considered what this would do to the center's reputation. Would he have to shoulder the blame? He was in charge, so it would probably fall on him, whether he was to blame or not.

"They're concerned. Upset? I'm not sure."

Grady opened the closet. It was empty. "Doesn't Mr. Corbin have clothes?"

Nancy peered into the closet. "Oh, my, he must've taken them with him."

Grady continued to search the room. Finally, he noticed a handprint on the window. "Do these windows open?"

"I suppose, but no one opens them in this wing because it would trigger the alarm in the nurses' station. Like this." Nancy opened the window. Nothing happened. She turned and looked at Grady. "He must've climbed out the window. I have no idea why the alarm didn't go off."

"We'll figure that out later. Right now we've got to find Mr. Corbin before something happens to him."

Amanda hung up the phone and looked at Kelsey. "You know, if you moved a little faster you'd probably be done dusting. I'm finished vacuuming."

Kelsey stopped and put a hand on one hip. "Faster isn't always better. My dusting lasts."

"Yeah, right. Like any dusting lasts."

"Who was on the phone?"

"Dad. He said they're still looking for that guy. He doesn't know when he'll be home, so we're supposed to fix lunch when we want to eat."

Kelsey shrugged. "So we probably won't get to go to Spokane."

"Probably not," Amanda said as she left the bedroom. She hurriedly put away the vacuum and the rest of the cleaning supplies. Then she flung herself onto the sofa and turned on the TV with the remote. After going through the channels several times, she shut off the TV and released a heavy sigh. "Kelsey, are you finally done?" Loud clanging came from the kitchen. "What are you doing?

"I'm going to bake cookies like Maria showed me."

Amanda hopped up from the couch and hurried into the kitchen. She found Kelsey setting bowls on the counter. "You can't do that while Dad's gone. You might burn down the house."

"No, I won't."

"You know what Dad said. No cooking unless a grown-up is here."

"How come you're telling me what to do? You don't always do what Dad says. So how come I have to?"

"Because Dad put me in charge." Amanda grabbed the bowls and started putting them away. She hated being in charge. Too much pressure to do the right things. But she wasn't going to let Kelsey know that.

"Well, I don't want you to be in charge." Kelsey plopped down on one of the chairs at the kitchen table. "If we can't cook, what do we do for lunch? I'm hungry."

"Peanut-butter sandwiches."

Kelsey wrinkled her nose. "I'm tired of peanut butter."

"Check the fridge for lunch meat."

Kelsey opened the refrigerator and stood there hanging on the door. "Hot dogs. Can I cook one in the microwave?"

"Yeah, microwave's okay. Cook me one, too."

Minutes later, Amanda joined Kelsey at the table, where they ate hot dogs smothered in ketchup and munched on carrots.

"I'm so glad I get this cast off on Monday. My arm's starting to itch."

"It's about time. That thing looks really nasty."

"Don't pick on me." Kelsey stuck her tongue out. "I wish Maria still lived upstairs. We could go visit her instead of being bored."

"Let's do it."

"Do what?"

"Visit Maria."

"But she lives out in the country. It's too far to walk out there," Kelsey protested. "Besides, she's mad at Dad."

"But she's not mad at us and it's not much farther than the walkathon we did for the Heart Association at school."

"Really?"

"Yeah. We can surprise her."

"You know how to get there?"

"Yeah, it's easy. I even know a shortcut."

"Shouldn't we tell her we're coming?"

Amanda shook her head. "No, then it won't be a surprise. Besides, we want Dad and Maria to get back together, don't we?"

"Yeah, but—"

"But nothing. He'll have to come get us. And he'll have to see Maria."

"I don't know. It might not be a good idea."

"Well, I'm going whether you do or not." Amanda got up and put her dishes in the dishwasher. Maybe doing this would teach her dad not to keep breaking his promises. He'd come home and wonder where they were.

"You can't leave me," Kelsey whined. "I'll tell Dad."

"Go ahead. I don't care."

Kelsey hung her head, then looked up at Amanda. "Okay, I'll go, but you have to promise not to walk too fast and leave me behind."

"I won't do that, Kels." Amanda gave Kelsey's shoulders a squeeze. "We're in this together."

Chapter Fifteen

Grady barely touched the gas pedal as he drove his car along the streets near the assisted-living center. His gaze searched up and down and in between the houses. There was no sign of Henry Corbin. He stopped to ask a passerby whether he had seen an older man walking in the neighborhood. He hadn't.

Since none of the nurses or aides was sure how long the man had been gone, it was difficult to determine how far he had gotten. Where would he go? Maybe Henry himself had no idea.

Grady remembered Jillian telling him how her mom had driven to town one day, become disoriented and tried to walk home. She had gotten lost. He just had to find the man before something terrible happened.

Grady was tempted to pray. It was something he hadn't done in a long time, but he'd been thinking a lot about God lately. Ever since Beth had talked to him. Ever since the girls had gotten him to go to church. And ever since he'd realized how much he cared for Maria.

He wasn't sure whether God was going to listen to him, but it was worth a try.

God, please help us find Henry Corbin unharmed.

Grady's cell phone rang. The lighted screen indicated a call from his office. Maybe they had found Henry. "Hello."

His thoughts plummeted when he learned that no one had located Henry and that his family had arrived. Dreading the meeting, he drove back to the assisted-living facility. When he was just a few blocks from the center, his cell phone rang again. Hoping it meant someone had found the missing resident, he grabbed his phone and answered it. "Grady Reynolds—"

"Dad…" Amanda's one-word cry disintegrated into garbled nonsense.

"Amanda, I can't understand you." Grady strained to make out her words as more distorted sounds came over the phone.

"Dad, can you hear me?"

Grady was relieved to hear Amanda's voice again, but his relief was short-lived when he recognized the sound of fear in her tone. "Yes, yes. Is something wrong?"

"We're lost!" Amanda cried.

"Lost? How can you be lost? Aren't you at home?"

Sniffles sounded over the phone. "Please don't be angry."

"Why should I be angry?" More garbled noises. "Amanda. Amanda, I can't hear you anymore. Amanda!"

Silence.

Grady turned off the engine and got out of the car in hopes of regaining the phone signal, even though he knew his wasn't the signal that was lost. He paced next to his car. "Amanda?"

"Dad, we need help." The words crackled into the phone.

"What's going on?" His mind roiled with frustration, foreboding and fear. "Tell me what's wrong."

"We're lost out here in the woods."

"The woods?"

"Yes, we were going to Maria's."

Grady ran a hand through his hair as he tried to make sense of what Amanda was saying. "Why?"

"Because…tired…waiting…you." Her voice cut in and out.

"Do you have any idea where you are? What road did you take?"

"I don't know," Amanda cried. "I…" The rest of the sentence trailed away in faint crackling.

"Amanda."

Silence again.

Grady alternately listened and called Amanda's name. Nothing. He waited and finally hung up and hit the speed dial for Amanda's cell phone. He was immediately put into her phone's voice mail. His brow wrinkled as he tried to think. For a moment panic froze him. He couldn't think. He couldn't move. He couldn't function.

Then Grady remembered Henry Corbin. His job. For too long he had buried himself in his work to ease the pain of Nina's betrayal and death. Even though he had tried to change, he had let work rob him of the love of another woman. He had let work override time with his children. He couldn't lose them, too. There was only one choice. He had to find his kids, even if it meant losing his job.

Grady called Nancy as he got back into his car. She answered as he drove out of town toward Maria's in search of Amanda and Kelsey. "Nancy, this is Grady. Tell the Corbins I'm sorry, but I can't meet with them now. Something's come up with my kids and they need me. The police will take care of the search for Henry. Call me when you find him."

Nancy didn't question his departure and said she would deliver his message. Next, he punched in Maria's number. She answered on the third ring. Her voice brought a little warmth to his heart, which was frozen with fear for his girls.

"Maria, this is Grady. Please talk to me," he said, hoping she wouldn't hang up. "Have you heard from Amanda or Kelsey today?"

"No, why?"

With worry pressing down on his chest until he could barely talk, Grady did his best to explain the situation.

"You mean they were trying to hike to my house and got lost?"

"As far as I could make out from the bad phone transmission. And it's all my fault. I promised them—"

Maria interrupted him. "Blaming yourself won't help now. Have you called the sheriff's department?"

"No, I wanted to check with you first in case you'd heard from them. I'll call."

"And I'll call Pastor Craig and see if he can organize a group to help search."

"I'm driving out to your place now, just in case I can see them on my way out there."

"I'll be waiting. And, Grady, I'll be praying, too."

"Thanks." *God, please don't let anything bad happen to my girls.* His stomach rumbled. He hadn't eaten anything since breakfast, but eating didn't matter. Finding his girls did. He gripped the steering wheel as he drove down the highway. Misery welled up inside him as his mind buzzed with thoughts about what had brought him to this point.

His job had been everything to him. He had used it to get over his grief about Nina. That had been his problem all along. His work had come before everything else. Not now. The only thing that mattered was finding Amanda and Kelsey. Work couldn't save him if something happened to those precious girls.

What good was a job if he didn't have his kids?

While he drove, he prayed. *God, I know I've strayed far from You. I've questioned Your existence. I've blamed You for everything that's gone wrong in my life, and now I know I'm the one to blame. So I don't know why You'd listen to me and answer my prayer, but I'm asking for Your forgiveness and a whole lot of help here. I realize that I need You. My life can't be right without You. Please, Lord, bring my girls back to me. Keep them safe.*

Maria stood at her front door as she watched for Grady. Her mind swirled with questions. Why had the girls decided to hike to her house? How had they become lost if they had been walking along the main roads? And how was she going to react to being with Grady again? But when his car appeared, the last question didn't need to be answered. She hurried out to greet him.

When he emerged from the car, she read the deep concern in his eyes. "Thank you for talking to me and letting me come over. Have you heard anything?"

"I called Pastor Craig. He started the prayer chain. Clay called and he's organizing some volunteers. Did you talk to the sheriff's department?" She wanted to reach out and comfort him, but his greeting had made her realize that she had created a huge gulf between them. This was not the time to worry about their relationship. This was all about his lost children.

"Is it all right if I come in?"

"Absolutely," she replied, wounded that he had to ask. "Please tell me what you know."

"Not much. That became very evident when the guy from the sheriff's department starting asking me questions." He sighed and ran his hand through his hair as he paced back and forth in the living room. "I couldn't tell them what time the girls had left home, what they were wearing or what they had with them, other than a cell phone that doesn't get a signal where they are. That's about the only clue we've got."

"Are you meeting with someone from there?"

"Yes, they're coming here. I hope that's okay." His eyes pleaded for understanding.

"Whatever it takes to find Amanda and Kelsey."

His look of anguish made her feel as though a large hand was pressing down on her chest. He had no idea how miserable she'd been without him the past week. Only a week had passed since their argument, but it seemed like forever. Despite the heartache, she had determined that she just couldn't deal with his workaholic tendencies. But being with him again undermined her whole thought process.

Before either of them could say anything else, the doorbell rang. Several people from the sheriff's department had arrived. While Grady talked with them, Clay, Beth and Max came, followed by Sam and Jillian and several others from church. The group waited quietly in the living room while Grady talked with the group of uniformed men. Then, in a flurry of activity, they made calls and began to execute a search-and-rescue plan.

Grady stepped into the living room.

"Do you need our help?" Clay greeted Grady with a hug, something Maria wished she could do.

Grady shook his head. "Right now they'd rather send in the professionals. They'll use helicopters to search the area. And they're going to check with the phone companies to determine which tower Amanda's phone signal came from."

"That sounds helpful."

"Even though I didn't think I'd be much help, they used my information to determine an approximate area where they are going to search." Grady released a heavy sigh. "I just don't understand why the girls didn't stay on the main roads."

Max stood up. "I might know."

"How?" Grady asked as everyone in the room looked at Max.

"One night, after practice at church, Amanda had me drive out here, so she could show me Maria's new house." Worry covered Max's face as he gazed at Grady. "And I told them about the shortcut from the main highway that goes up through that wooded area. Maybe they tried to take that."

"Max, you've got to give the officers this information. It may help them narrow the search area."

"Sure." Max followed Grady to the command post that had been set up in Maria's basement.

When they returned, Clay asked, "Was that information helpful?"

Nodding, Grady began pacing the floor again. "But I'm worried. It's beginning to rain and the wind has picked up. The windchill is near thirty degrees already, and it's only supposed to get colder when it clears. We have to find them before nightfall. Hypothermia. If they're out there too long in this bad weather, they might get hypothermia. If anything happens to them, I'll never forgive myself." He buried his face in his hands, then looked back at Clay. "I should be out there searching, too."

"It's not going to do you any good to go out there and get lost, yourself," Beth said, giving him a hug.

"I know. I know. But I feel so helpless."

Clay put one arm around Grady's shoulders. "Leave it in God's hands."

"That's hard to do sometimes, but I know now it's the best choice—thanks to all of you who've been praying for me, especially Beth." Looking at his sister-in-law, Grady smiled for the first time. "Her testimony made me examine my life. And when everything started going wrong today, I knew I had to rely on God. I need Him in my life."

"We all do," Sam said. "Let's pray. It's the one thing we *can* do."

Maria took in Grady's affirmation of God with joy bubbling in her soul. But her joy faded when she saw the worry that still creased Grady's brow. She wanted to encourage him as Beth had, but he'd found a place on the opposite side of the circle, obviously avoiding the possibility that they might have to hold hands while they prayed. As she bowed her head, Maria realized she had pushed Grady away because she had been too judgmental, unlike Beth, who had used gentle words of persuasion to turn Grady toward God.

As they finished praying, big, fat drops of rain began to splatter against the windows in the living room. The tall pines in the wooded area behind the house swayed in the wind. Maria shivered as she thought of Amanda and Kelsey somewhere out in this storm. No wonder Grady was nearly wearing a path in her new carpet as he paced back and forth in front of the window. She wanted to reassure him and make things right between them, but this wasn't the time to be thinking about herself.

Time passed without any word. Light began to fade as night descended and the storm didn't abate. Her thoughts descended into despair, as well, and she began to blame herself for what had happened. If she hadn't been so hardheaded, she and Grady wouldn't have had their disagreement. The girls wouldn't have gone on this hike. They wouldn't be lost. The worry was driving her crazy. Hadn't they just prayed? Why worry when you can pray? That message just wasn't soaking into her brain. *Please, Lord, bring Amanda and Kelsey back to us.*

Loud footsteps shook Maria from her prayer. One of the uniformed men rushed up to Grady. "Your daughters have been found and they're being flown to Spokane."

"Are they going to be okay?" Grady asked, his voice choking back emotion.

The officer nodded. "They're suffering from hypothermia, but they're going to be okay."

Grady looked upward. "Thank you, God."

Tears sprang to Maria's eyes as she watched Grady. She wanted to share in his joy and show him support, but she wasn't sure he would welcome anything from her.

The emergency room pulsated with energy as nurses and doctors rushed to heal and save lives. The smell of antiseptics permeated the air. Beeping monitors reverberated off the walls as Maria hovered outside the room where Amanda and Kelsey were recuperating. All the other folks from Pinecrest had left when the doctors announced that the girls were doing well.

Maria remained, hoping to talk to Grady before she left, even though she wasn't sure what she would say. She wanted to make things right with him, but she didn't know how. She waited just outside the room as Grady stood with his back to the door while he talked with Amanda and Kelsey.

Kelsey's high-pitched voice carried into the hall. "Will Maria forgive us for causing so much trouble?"

"Of course she will." Grady's reply made Maria's heart twist.

"But she didn't forgive you, Daddy."

Kelsey's statement punched Maria in the gut. She shrank away from the door, nausea hitting her hard. Sick to the core, she stumbled into the waiting area, which was filled with the drone of a TV news program. She made her way to the little chapel where the group had prayed earlier. She fell on her knees as she came into the quiet room.

For a while, she couldn't think. She just absorbed the tranquility. Then the emotions and fears she had been holding in all day washed away in the tears flowing down her cheeks. *Dear Lord, I know You've promised to forgive us if we forgive others. Thank You for showing me I haven't been doing what You've asked of me.*

While she prayed, she wondered about the message she had given Grady's girls with her unforgiving attitude. She remembered the Bible story where Peter asked how many times he should forgive his brother. Jesus said, "I tell you not seven times, but seventy-seven times."

She hadn't even forgiven Grady once, much less

seventy-seven times. How could she forgive herself for being so foolish? Loving meant forgiving—forgiving endlessly. She loved Grady. She loved his girls. Had she thrown away her chance at happiness? Being with them was more important than time for herself would ever be. She had to tell him and ask for his forgiveness.

Grady preserved the scene in his mind—his daughters in hospital beds—so that whenever he thought of putting his job before his family, he would remember what he had almost lost. Maybe this picture would keep him from making that mistake again.

He bowed his head. *God, I don't know what my future holds, but I need You in it. I want to share my life with Maria. Give me the words and the actions that would make that possible.*

"Daddy, I want to see Maria." Kelsey's sweet little voice made him look up.

"I'll get her." Grady stepped into the waiting area of the emergency room. He was sure he'd seen her after everyone else had left, but he didn't see her now. When he spied the reception desk, he walked to it. "Have you seen an attractive dark-haired woman?"

The woman behind the desk pointed down the hall. "I thought I saw a woman with dark hair go in that direction."

With every nerve wired, he went down the corridor until he came to the chapel. Something told him he'd find Maria there. He slowly pushed the door open and entered. Quiet darkness surrounded him, and it took a moment for his eyes to adjust.

The faint glow that illuminated the small table at the front also cast a light on a kneeling figure. Squinting into the dimness, Grady recognized Maria. He wanted to say something, but he feared frightening her. Just as he opened his mouth to speak, she looked up.

Even in the low light, he could see the tears gleaming in her eyes.

"Maria."

"Grady."

They both spoke at once.

When she stood and walked toward him, he met her halfway. "Maria…can you give me another chance? I—"

She pressed a finger to his lips as she stepped closer. "I'm the one who needs the second chance. I'm the one who needs forgiveness."

He took her hand in his. "Why? I'm the one who messed up."

"No, I am. I heard what Kelsey said about forgiving. I didn't forgive you, and I'm so sorry." She blinked and a tear rolled down one cheek. She brushed it away.

Grady took her hand and brought it to his lips. He tasted the salt from her tears. "Let me tell you what I learned today." He took a shaky breath and gave her an account of Henry Corbin's escape. "I realized then that nothing's more important than my family. It took having to choose to make me realize something I should've known all along."

Maria looked up at him. "I hope they found Mr. Corbin."

Chuckling, Grady nodded. "Nancy called me and told me that they found him about two miles from the center. He was carrying his clothes on hangers while he roamed down the street in his underwear. Thankfully, they found him before it rained, or he might have ended up in here with Amanda and Kelsey."

"Poor Mr. Corbin. He must've been cold." Maria tried to stifle a chuckle. "I shouldn't laugh, but it does paint a humorous picture."

"The girls are asking to see you."

"I want to see them, too."

"Before we go, I have something to tell you." Holding her hands, he gazed into her eyes and hoped she'd understand what he was trying to say. "All that's happened has made me realize that every day is precious and that we can't count on tomorrow. I know this is sudden, but I want to spend all the tomorrows God gives me with you. I love you, Maria. Will you be part of our family?"

"Is this a proposal?"

"Yes. If you need more time—"

"I don't need more time. I love you, too."

"That's a relief." He grinned.

"You thought I might say no?"

"I considered that possibility."

"Haven't we had this conversation before?"

He squeezed her hands. "Kind of, but this time I know where my priorities lie." Grady pulled her into his arms and kissed her. Then he held her at arm's length. "We should tell Amanda and Kelsey our news. But be careful—Kelsey might start planning the wedding."

Maria giggled as they walked arm in arm. "That might be interesting. What do you think? Hot dogs for the reception?"

"A good chance, if she's in charge of the menu."

When they entered Amanda and Kelsey's hospital room, Maria stood between the two beds and reached out her hands. Amanda grabbed one and Kelsey the other. The three females all began talking at once. Grady watched, happiness wrapping around him. He saw his days full of welcoming kisses, warm hugs and wonderful laughter.

Finally, Maria drew him into the circle, and Grady knew that the awesome God he had doubted was filling his life with more love than he ever could have imagined.

Dear Reader,

Thank you for reading *The Heart's Forgiveness,* the last of my stories set in Pinecrest, Washington. Although the little town is fictional, the area in which it is set, near Spokane, is very real and dear to my heart. I lived there when I was in high school, and two of my brothers Greg and George, still live in and around Spokane.

I hope you enjoyed reading about Grady and Maria on their journey to the forgiveness that brought them love. They learned how to deal with life's troubles and forgive each other with God's help. Facing difficult times is something we all face in life, but God's comfort and forgiveness can help us cope.

I enjoy hearing from readers. You can write to me at mwhren@bellsouth.net or P.O. Box 16461, Fernandina Beach, Florida 32035. Please visit my Web site at www.merrilleewhren.com.

May God bless you,

Merrillee Whren

QUESTIONS FOR DISCUSSION

1. At the beginning of the story Maria dreads meeting Grady. Why does she feel this way? Was there a time when you felt uncomfortable meeting someone? Why? How did you deal with it?

2. Grady believes that Maria had a part in his dead wife's betrayal. How does he learn he was wrong? Is it always easy to face the truth? Why or why not? Have you ever misjudged someone's actions? How did you learn the truth? What happened as a result?

3. Even though Maria and Grady have some unresolved issues, they have to work together. What do they do to solve the issues? Have you or anyone you know ever been in a situation where a coworker created a problem? How was it resolved?

4. Grady's daughters are very different. What difficulties does he have to deal with because of this? Do you have children or know of others who have children with very different personalities? Has this posed any problems?

5. Throughout the story, Maria sees that Grady is trying to make some changes in his life, but he continually falls back into his old habits. Why do you suppose this happens? Have you or someone you know tried to make a change in your life? Did you or they succeed? Why or why not?

6. Grady has a problem trusting God. Why? Have there ever been circumstances in your life or someone else's life that have caused you to doubt God? What reassurances do we have that God is working in our lives?

7. Maria is constantly drawn into the lives of Grady and his daughters. Why does she resist? Why does she feel God's calling in her relationship with-them? Have you ever felt that God was calling you to help someone? Explain. What do James 1:27 and 1 Peter 4:8-10 say about helping others?

8. Amanda has some problems that Grady must address. What are they? Why do you think he is afraid to confront them? Do you think he did the right thing? How would you have dealt with these problems?

9. Grady realizes he has put his work before his family. What brings him to that realization? What can you do to make sure you have your priorities in the right order? What does the Bible say about what should be important in your life? Read Matthew 6:33, Matthew 19:29-30 and Luke 12:16-21.

10. What does Kelsey say that makes Maria see she hasn't treated Grady the way God wants her to? What story from the Bible does Maria recall? Read Matthew 17:21-35 and Luke 17:4. What do these scriptures teach about forgiving others?

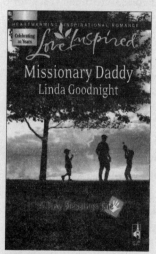

REQUEST YOUR FREE BOOKS!

2 FREE INSPIRATIONAL NOVELS
PLUS 2
FREE
MYSTERY GIFTS

Love Inspired®

YES! Please send me 2 FREE Love Inspired® novels and my 2 FREE mystery gifts. After receiving them, if I don't wish to receive any more books, I can return the shipping statement marked "cancel." If I don't cancel, I will receive 4 brand-new novels every month and be billed just $3.99 per book in the U.S., or $4.74 per book in Canada, plus 25¢ shipping and handling per book and applicable taxes, if any*. That's a savings of 20% off the cover price! I understand that accepting the 2 free books and gifts places me under no obligation to buy anything. I can always return a shipment and cancel at any time. Even if I never buy another book from Steeple Hill, the two free books and gifts are mine to keep forever.

113 IDN EF26   313 IDN EF27

Name _____ (PLEASE PRINT) _____

Address _____ Apt. # _____

City _____ State/Prov. _____ Zip/Postal Code _____

Signature (if under 18, a parent or guardian must sign) _____

Order online at www.LoveInspiredBooks.com

Or mail to Steeple Hill Reader Service™:

IN U.S.A.: P.O. Box 1867, Buffalo, NY 14240-1867
IN CANADA: P.O. Box 609, Fort Erie, Ontario L2A 5X3

Not valid to current Love Inspired subscribers.

Want to try two free books from another series?
Call 1-800-873-8635 or visit www.morefreebooks.com

* Terms and prices subject to change without notice. NY residents add applicable sales tax. Canadian residents will be charged applicable provincial taxes and GST. This offer is limited to one order per household. All orders subject to approval. Credit or debit balances in a customer's account(s) may be offset by any other outstanding balance owed by or to the customer. Please allow 4 to 6 weeks for delivery.

Your Privacy: Steeple Hill is committed to protecting your privacy. Our Privacy Policy is available online at www.eHarlequin.com or upon request from the Reader Service. From time to time we make our lists of customers available to reputable firms who may have a product or service of interest to you. If you would prefer we not share your name and address, please check here. ☐

LIREG07

Love Inspired

TITLES AVAILABLE NEXT MONTH

Don't miss these four stories in August

IN HIS DREAMS by Gail Gaymer Martin
Escape to beautiful Beaver Island could be the answer to
Marsha Sullivan's problems. Since her husband's death, Marsha
had lost her way, but being with her widowed brother-in-law Jeff
and his daughter made her feel like part of a family once again.

MISSIONARY DADDY by Linda Goodnight
A Tiny Blessings Tale

Samantha Harcourt never forgot the handsome missionary she
met abroad, but she never expected to see him in Chestnut Grove.
He was trying to find homes for the world's orphans, including
two he's crazy about. Could Samantha help Eric Pellegrino make a
loving home for the four of them?

THE COLOR OF COURAGE by Patricia Davids
Only faith sustained Lindsey Mandel after the loss of her beloved
twin brother. Now a freak accident would test the U.S. Army
corporal's mettle once again. Desperate to save her brother's
injured horse, Lindsey would have to put her trust in handsome
veterinarian Brian Cutter.

TRUSTING HIM by Brenda Minton
Since the day he left prison, Michael Carson sought a second
chance. Working alongside youth leader Maggie Simmons
seemed like the perfect plan. Michael prayed he could resist old
temptations and keep God—and Maggie—close to his heart.

LICNM0707